THEORY

OF THE

MORAL LIFE

BY

JOHN DEWEY

WITH AN INTRODUCTION BY

ARNOLD ISENBERG
Stanford University

�֎IRVINGTON PUBLISHERS, Inc., New York

EDITOR'S FOREWORD

EXCEPT for the "Authors' Introduction" following these prefatory pages, this volume is a redaction pure and simple of Part II of Dewey and Tufts' *Ethics*, from the revised edition of 1932. The present foreword means to give such reasons as are deemed necessary for the republication, in this centennial year of Dewey's birth, of that portion of the book. I could make short work of apologies and explanations by pointing out that the present edition, truncated (though not abridged) as it is, is only a natural and timely tribute to the memory of the great philosopher. For while (*a*) there is scarcely a chapter or a page that Dewey ever wrote that does not subsume itself under the heading of moral ("practical") philosophy in some more or less extended use of the phrase, yet (*b*) from the earliest days of his career he set himself to inditing papers, outlines, and textbooks belonging to ethics in that stricter and narrower sense which does not comprehend, for example, *How We Think* or the finely moralistic *Quest for Certainty*—and which comprehends only doubtfully Dewey's chief treatise on pedagogy, *Democracy and Education*. But (*c*) among the books and the innumerable articles which do devote themselves to the problems of ethics, none is *at once* so complete, as is this introductory textbook intended for use in class, in its spread over long-outstanding and recognized issues of moral philosophy, so thorough in its examination of these issues, and so finally expressive of the positions at which the mature philosopher had arrived.[1] Let us add, to his honor, that Dewey—from his earliest years of manhood a teacher, an "educationist," even a pedant—scarcely understood the difference between a book addressed to the profession, another addressed to the laity, and a third intended for the instruction of college freshmen. Some passages, befitting the difficulty of their subjects, are more difficult than others; some, too, are exceptionally difficult because Dewey has not seen quite

[1] *Human Nature and Conduct*, published between the first and the second editions of Dewey and Tufts, takes similar positions wherever it overlaps with the latter in theme. And it has many a vigorous critical excursus upon evils of modern society and errors of modern thought. It is perhaps better in its presentation of the material to be found in Chapter II of the present volume. But it omits the fundamental points of contention that are treated here in Chapters IV, V, and VI.

through his subject; but all alike, and in equal measure, represent a student talking to students, a philosopher to philosophers, and a vexed human being to his fellows. I have found, accordingly, that on being asked for advice, "What to read first?", I could say nothing but "Jump in anywhere," mentally adding that if it were the *Logic*, there would be a drowning for which, however, the victim would be none the worse. And as to Dewey and Tufts in particular: For ten years I "used" this book, successfully, in classes liberally sprinkled with freshmen and sophomores. But when a candidate for the doctor's degree asks me how best to prepare —always, in an incredibly short time—for the Qualifying Examination in Ethics and Theory of Value, I find nothing better to say than: "You know some Aristotle? You're up on Hume and on Kant? Very well. Read the *Principia Ethica;* or reread it, carefully. And read Part II of Dewey and Tufts, *carefully*." [2]

So much by way of elaborating upon an opinion held by the editor: that a certain group of some one hundred and seventy pages embedded in an academic textbook in ethics is representative of the best efforts of a leading modern philosopher. To recur now to the facts about the present edition. In the first and the revised editions of Dewey and Tufts, the work is divided into three parts. Part I, written (as a preface informs us) by Professor Tufts, is entitled "The Beginnings and Growth of Morality." Its materials are drawn largely from history and ethnology. It is a kind of natural history of the moral sense, from the bare traces of reason and conscience in instinct and group life through some of their more articulate expressions in Israel, Greece, and Rome; its scope is very nearly coincident with what, in many a course syllabus and introductory text, is called the factual or pre-ethical "data of ethics." Part II, written by Dewey, bears the title "Theory of the Moral Life" and consists of six chapters including nearly everything in the joint work that falls within the province of what, in Dewey's day and our own, is termed with emphasis "*normative* ethics," "*moral philosophy*," or "ethical *theory*." In Part III, "The World of Action," which ventures to apply the lessons of moral theory to contemporaneous public questions (for example, individualism and collectivism, factory legislation, the Sherman Act, immigration, and the income tax), Dewey was responsible for two chapters and Tufts for five. The extent to which the book was a product of collaboration is indicated by a remark in the preface: ". . . each of the authors has con-

---

[2] If the available time is *more* than incredibly short, the best choice out of Dewey is Chapter X of *The Quest for Certainty.*

tributed suggestions and criticisms to the work of the other in a sufficient degree to make the book throughout a joint work." There is something, then, of Tufts in Dewey's share, which nevertheless remains Dewey's share.

Dewey's share has, moreover, been extracted from a matrix by which it was not very tightly bound. Part II *came at the right place* between Parts I and III; but it is in no way *dependent* for the coherence of its argument upon anything that comes before or after. The present selection is not "open-ended" at either end; it would be a disappointment to an editor if a good reader should form the opinion that it is.

Having thus shown why Part II can stand alone, I should perhaps give positive reasons for the omission of Parts I and III. Tufts' contribution in Part I has been surpassed by thirty or forty years of research in genetics, cultural anthropology, pre-history, ancient history, and above all descriptive ethics; for it is possible nowadays to know much more than he could know about the systems and fragments of traditionally engrained doctrine that have prevailed in parts of the world. It would be unfair to say that Tufts is "dated," since he can still be read with profit; but for anyone who seeks this profit there is always Dewey and Tufts, still in print and still available in most of the larger libraries in the country.

Dewey's and Tufts' chapters in Part III would not, on the other hand, strike anyone—except perhaps the historian of the very recent past—as outmoded by the results of research. They are interesting as well as profitable. But they do presume on the part of the reader (what I think should not be presumed in a student in contemporary courses in ethics) a beguiling interest in the issues by which a previous generation was beset: relatively dead issues like the direct election of Senators, the graduated income tax, prohibition, and women's suffrage and relatively lively issues set, however, in an archaic context—individualism and collectivism, liberty of thought and expression, nationalism, peace and war. The serious student of Dewey will take the pains to read all or most of Part III. But it is the second part alone that seems to me to retain all the vitality and trenchancy that it had when I read it first, in 1932.

There remains a word to be said to instructors in ethics. Our objective—publisher's and editor's—has been to produce a handy as well as a lively book for class use. If Dewey and Tufts, once and for long the standard text in the field, has fallen out of favor in the last decade or two, this denotes no sudden or gradual depreciation of Dewey's achievement. It means only that other ways are being tried of meeting the instructor's perennial problem. What is the problem of the instructor in ethics? He would like to read—and have his class read—one author at some length, someone who undertakes to traverse the field; in effect, then, a textbook. But he would not like to be forced, by the size of the textbook and by its price, to oust all those other authors, historical and modern, who are represented in such a useful anthology as Melden's *Ethical Theories* and in a variety of classics available in paperback. I make bold to say that the present volume by Dewey, if unaccompanied and uninterspersed with other readings, would produce on the average student the effect of monotony. But the book of readings, with no single standard author to refer it to, imposes a truly fearful strain on instructor and student: how to see in this collection an organized subject with authors facing one another across a small number of boundaries, not too thick and rough. (I believe this was once—and in esthetics still is—called the problem of unity and variety.) Dewey's text, which is certainly not devoid of internal variety, is nevertheless being offered to instructors as a binding medium by which the colors of the great moralists can all, so far as a semester permits, be held together. The six chapters survey, with reasonable thoroughness, a greater cluster of interlocked issues in ethics than does the usual assignment in Aristotle, Augustine, Hobbes, Butler, Hume, Kant, Bentham, Sidgwick, or Moore. They thus provide a stimulating companion text for the course in ethics.

The editor's work has proved remarkably easy. Critical as I might be, on grounds of style or substance, of one page or another passage, I have found no warrant for altering a single sentence in the edition of 1932 and none—it is needless to say—for editorial editions' or interpolations. Nor would a text which accomplishes so largely its own purpose of introducing the reader to moral philosophy benefit by an attempt to explain Dewey's meaning in footnotes. Should a phrase or a paragraph seem unclear, the right thing to do is to read it again and, if it should still seem unclear, to read it again. Correction, therefore, has been confined to some previously unnoticed misprints and to the fixing up of an occasional reference (chiefly in the bibliographies) backward or forward to Part I or Part III of Dewey and Tufts.

I am indebted to Charlotte Furth for assistance with the editing.

A. I.

Stanford, California
February 16, 1960

CONTENTS

Introduction   viii

I. The Nature of Moral Theory   3

II. Ends, the Good and Wisdom   29

III. Right, Duty, and Loyalty   64

IV. Approbation, the Standard and Virtue   89

V. Moral Judgment and Knowledge   120

VI. The Moral Self   147

INTRODUCTION *

§ 1. DEFINITION AND METHODS

THE place for an accurate definition of a subject is at the
end of an inquiry rather than at the beginning, but a brief
definition will serve to mark out the field. Ethics is the science
that deals with conduct, in so far as this is considered as right
or wrong, good or bad. A single term for conduct so considered
is "moral conduct," or the "moral life." Another way of
stating the same thing is to say that ethics aims to give a
systematic account of our judgments about conduct, in so
far as these estimate it from the standpoint of right or wrong,
good or bad.

The terms "ethics" and "ethical" are derived from a Greek
word *ethos* which originally meant customs, usages, especially
those belonging to some group as distinguished from another,
and later came to mean disposition, character. They are thus
like the Latin word "moral," from *mores*, or the German
sittlich, from *Sitten*. As we shall see, it was in customs, "ethos,"
"mores," that the moral or ethical began to appear. For
customs were not merely habitual ways of acting; they were
ways approved by the group or society. To act contrary to the
customs of the group brought severe disapproval. This might
not be formulated in precisely our terms—right and wrong,
good and bad,—but the attitude was the same in essence. The
terms ethical and moral as applied to the conduct of today
imply of course a far more complex and advanced type of life
than the old words "ethos" and "mores," just as economics
deals with a more complex problem than "the manage-
ment of a household," but the terms have a distinct value
if they suggest the way in which the moral life had its beginning.

To give a scientific account of judgments about conduct,
means to find the principles which are the basis of these judgments. Conduct or the moral life has two obvious aspects.
On the one hand it is a life of purpose. It implies thought and

* From *Ethics;* pp. 3–5, 6–9.

viii

feeling, ideals and motives, valuation and choice. These are processes to be studied by psychological methods. On the other hand, conduct has its outward side. It has relations to nature, and especially to human society. Moral life is called out or stimulated by certain necessities of individual and social existence. As Protagoras put it, in mythical form, the gods gave men a sense of justice and of reverence, in order to enable them to unite for mutual preservation.[1] And in turn the moral life aims to modify or transform both natural and social environments, to build a "kingdom of man" which shall be also an ideal social order—a "kingdom of God." These relations to nature and society are studied by the biological and social sciences. Sociology, economics, politics, law, and jurisprudence deal particularly with this aspect of conduct. Ethics must employ their methods and results for this aspect of its problem, as it employs psychology for the examination of conduct on its inner side.

But ethics is not merely the sum of these various sciences. It has a problem of its own which is created by just this twofold aspect of life and conduct. It has to relate these two sides. It has to study the inner process *as determined by the outer conditions or as changing these outer conditions*, and the outward behavior or institution *as determined by the inner purpose, or as affecting the inner life*. To study choice and purpose is psychology; to study choice as affected by the rights of others and to judge it as right or wrong by this standard is ethics. Or again, to study a corporation may be economics, or sociology, or law; to study its activities as resulting from the purposes of persons or as affecting the welfare of persons, and to judge its acts as good or bad from such a point of view, is ethics. . . .

§ 2. THE MORAL AS A GROWTH

At present biologists, psychologists, and sociologists are far from agreement as to the relative part played in the individ-

[1] Plato, *Protagoras*, pp. 320 ff.

ual's make-up and character by heredity, environment, and the individual's own choices and habits. Similarly in the history of races and cultures, the importance of race, of economic and other social forces, and of great men, is variously estimated by anthropologists, historians, and other students of this complex problem. For our purpose we shall assume that all these factors enter into moral growth, although it may sometimes be convenient to distinguish what nature does, what society does, and what the individual does for himself, as he chooses, thinks, selects, and forms habits and character.

We may also find it convenient to distinguish *three levels* of behavior and conduct: (1) behavior which is motived by various biological, economic, or other non-moral impulses or needs (e.g., family, life, work), and which yet has important results for morals; (2) behavior or conduct in which the individual accepts with relatively little critical reflection the standards and ways of his group as these are embodied in customs or *mores;* (3) conduct in which the individual thinks and judges for himself, considers whether a purpose is good or right, decides and chooses, and does not accept the standards of his group without reflection.

Although this separate consideration of these levels has convenience in gaining clear conceptions of stages and factors in moral growth, it is important to remember that no individual of maturity is wholly at any single level. We are all born into families; we all pursue activities which develop thinking; we all are members of some social group and are subtly molded by its standards; we all on some occasions think and choose.

If, instead of considering separately the factors and forces in moral growth, we look at the process of growth as it now goes on in a child, and as to some extent it has gone on in the history of those peoples which have had most to do with the present moral life of Europe and America, we may describe this as a process in which man becomes more *rational,* more *social*, and finally more *moral*. We examine briefly each of these aspects.

The first need of the organism is to live and grow. The first impulses and activities are therefore for food, self-defense, and other immediate necessities. Primitive men eat, sleep, fight, build shelters, and give food and protection to their offspring. The rationalizing process will mean at first greater use of intelligence to satisfy these same wants. It will show itself in skilled occupations, in industry and trade, in the utilizing of all resources to further man's power and happiness. But to rationalize conduct is also to introduce new ends. It not only enables man to get what he wants; it changes the kind of objects that he wants. This shows itself externally in what man makes and in how he occupies himself. He must of course have food and shelter. But he makes temples and statues and poems. He makes myths and theories of the world. He carries on great enterprises in commerce or government, not so much to gratify desires for bodily wants as to experience the growth of power. He creates a family life which is raised to a higher level by art and religion. He does not live by bread only, but builds up gradually a life of reason. Psychologically this means that whereas at the beginning we want what our body calls for, we soon come to want things which the mind takes an interest in. As we form by memory, imagination, and reason a more continuous, permanent, highly-organized self, we require a far more permanent and ideal kind of good to satisfy us. This gives rise to the contrast between the material and ideal selves, or in another form, between the world and the spirit.

The socializing side of the process of development stands for an increased capacity to enter into relations with other human beings. Like the growth of reason it is both a means and an end. It has its roots in certain biological facts—sex, parenthood, kinship—and in the necessities of mutual support and protection. But the associations thus formed imply a great variety of activities which call out new powers and set up new ends. Language is one of the first of these activities and a first step toward more complete socialization. Coöperation, in all kinds of enterprises, interchange of services and goods, participation in social arts, associations for various purposes, institutions of blood, family, government, and religion, all add enormously to the individual's power. On the other hand, as he enters into these relations and becomes a member of all these bodies, he inevitably undergoes a transformation in his interests. Psychologically the process is one of building up a social self. Imitation and·suggestion, sympathy and affection, common purpose and common interest, are the aids in building such a self. As the various impulses, emotions, and purposes are more definitely organized into such a unit, it becomes possible to set off the interests of others against those interests that center in my more individual good. Conscious egoism and altruism become possible. The interests of self and others can be raised to the plane of rights and justice.

All this is not yet moral progress in the fullest sense. The progress to more rational and more social conduct is the indispensable condition of the moral, but not the whole story. What is needed is that the more rational and social conduct should itself be valued as good, and so be chosen and sought; or in terms of control, that the law which society or reason prescribes should be consciously thought of as right, used as a standard, and respected as binding. This gives the contrast between the higher and lower, as a conscious aim, not merely as a matter of taste. It raises the collision between self and others to the plane of personal rights and justice, of deliberate selfishness or benevolence. Finally it gives the basis for such organization of the social and rational choices that the progress already gained may be permanently secured in terms of acquired habit and character, while the attention, the struggle between duty and inclination, the conscious choice, move forward to a new issue. . . .

THEORY OF THE MORAL LIFE

GENERAL LITERATURE

Among the works which have had the most influence upon the development of the theory of morals are: Plato, dialogues entitled *Republic, Laws, Protagoras* and *Gorgias;* Aristotle, *Ethics;* Cicero, *De Finibus* and *De Officiis;* Marcus Aurelius, *Meditations;* Epictetus, *Conversations;* Lucretius, *De Rerum Natura;* St. Thomas Aquinas (selected and translated by Rickaby under title of *Aquinas Ethicus*); Hobbes, *Leviathan;* Spinoza, *Ethics;* Shaftesbury, *Characteristics,* and *Inquiry concerning Virtue;* Hutcheson, *System of Moral Philosophy;* Butler, *Sermons;* Hume, *Essays, Principles of Morals;* Adam Smith, *Theory of Moral Sentiments;* Bentham, *Principles of Morals and Legislation;* Kant, *Critique of Practical Reason,* and *Foundations of the Metaphysics of Ethics;* Comte, "Social Physics" (in his *Course of Positive Philosophy*); Mill, *Utilitarianism;* Spencer, *Principles of Ethics;* Green, *Prolegomena to Ethics;* Sidgwick, *Methods of Ethics;* Selby-Bigge, *British Moralists,* 2 vols. (a convenient collection of selections).

CHAPTER I

THE NATURE OF MORAL THEORY

§ 1. REFLECTIVE MORALITY AND ETHICAL THEORY

THE intellectual distinction between customary and re-flective morality is clearly marked. The former places the standard and rules of conduct in ancestral habit; the latter appeals to conscience, reason, or to some principle which includes thought. The distinction is as important as it is definite, for it shifts the center of gravity in morality. Never-theless the distinction is relative rather than absolute. Some degree of reflective thought must' have entered occasionally into systems which in the main were founded on social wont and use, while in contemporary morals, even when the need of critical judgment is most recognized, there is an immense amount of conduct that is merely accommodated to social usage. In what follows we shall, accordingly, emphasize the difference in *principle* between customary and reflective morals rather than try to describe different historic and social epochs. In principle a revolution was wrought when Hebrew prophets and Greek seers asserted that conduct is not truly conduct unless it springs from the heart, from personal desires and affections, or from personal insight and rational choice.

The change was revolutionary not only because it displaced custom from the supreme position, but even more because it entailed the necessity of criticizing existing customs and in-stitutions from a new point of view. Standards which were regarded by the followers of tradition as the basis of duty and responsibility were denounced by prophet and philosopher as the source of moral corruption. These proclaimed the hollow-ness of outer conformity and insisted upon the cleansing of

3

the heart and the clarifying of the mind as preconditions of any genuinely good conduct.

One great source of the abiding interest which Greek thought has for the western world is that it records so clearly the struggle to make the transition from customary to reflective conduct. In the Platonic dialogues for example Socrates is represented as constantly raising the question of whether morals can be taught. Some other thinker (like Protagoras in the dialogue of that name) is brought in who points out that habituation to existing moral traditions is actually taught. Parents and teachers constantly admonish the young "pointing out that one act is just, another unjust; one honorable and another dishonorable; one holy and another unholy." When a youth emerges from parental tutelage, the State takes up the task, for "the community compels them to learn laws and to live after the pattern of the laws and not according to their own fancies."

In reply, Socrates raises the question of the foundations of such teaching, of its right to be termed a genuine teaching of virtue, and in effect points out the need of a morality which shall be stable and secure because based upon constant and universal principles. Parents and teachers differ in their injunctions and prohibitions; different communities have different laws; the same community changes its habits with time and with transformations of government. How shall we know who among the teachers, whether individuals or States, is right? Is there no basis for morals except this fluctuating one? It is not enough to praise and blame, reward and punish, enjoin and prohibit. The essence of morals, it is implied, is to know the reason for these customary instructions; to ascertain the criterion which insures their being just. And in other dialogues, it is frequently asserted that even if the mass must follow custom and law without insight, those who make laws and fix customs should have sure insight into enduring principles, or else the blind will be leading the blind.

No fundamental difference exists between systematic moral theory—the general theme of this Second Part of our study—and the reflection an individual engages in when he attempts to find general principles which shall direct and justify his conduct. Moral theory begins, in germ, when any one asks "Why should I act thus and not otherwise? Why is this right and that wrong? What right has any one to frown upon this way of acting and impose that other way? Children make at least a start upon the road of theory when they assert that the injunctions of elders are arbitrary, being simply a matter of superior position. Any adult enters the road when, in the presence of moral perplexity, of doubt as to what it is right or best to do, he attempts to find his way out through reflection which will lead him to some principle he regards as dependable.

Moral theory cannot emerge when there is positive belief as to what is right and what is wrong, for then there is no occasion for reflection. It emerges when men are confronted with situations in which different desires promise opposed goods and in which incompatible courses of action seem to be morally justified. Only such a conflict of good ends and of standards and rules of right and wrong calls forth personal inquiry into the bases of morals. A critical juncture may occur when a person, for example, goes from a protected home life into the stress of competitive business, and finds that moral standards which apply in one do not hold in the other. Unless he merely drifts, accommodating himself to whatever social pressure is uppermost, he will feel the conflict. If he tries to face it in thought, he will search for a reasonable principle by which to decide where the right really lies. In so doing he enters into the domain of moral theory, even if he does so unwittingly.

For what is called moral theory is but a more conscious and systematic raising of the question which occupies the mind of any one who in the face of moral conflict and doubt seeks a way out through reflection. In short, moral theory is but an extension of what is involved in all reflective morality. There are two kinds of moral struggle. One kind, and that the most emphasized in moral writings and lectures, is the conflict which takes place when an individual is tempted to do something which he is convinced is wrong. Such instances are important practically in the life of an individual, but they are not the occasion of moral theory. The employee of a bank who is tempted to embezzle funds may indeed try to argue himself into finding reasons why it would not be wrong for him to do it. But in such a case, he is not really thinking, but merely permitting his desire to govern his beliefs. There is no sincere doubt in his mind as to what he should do when he seeks to find some justification for what he has made up his mind to do.

Take, on the other hand, the case of a citizen of a nation which has just declared war on another country. He is deeply attached to his own State. He has formed habits of loyalty and of abiding by its laws, and now one of its decrees is that he shall support war. He feels in addition gratitude and affection for the country which has sheltered and nurtured him. But he believes that this war is unjust, or perhaps he has a conviction that all war is a form of murder and hence wrong. One side of his nature, one set of convictions and habits, leads him to acquiesce in war; another deep part of his being protests. He is torn between two duties: he experiences a conflict between the incompatible values presented to him by his habits of citizenship and by his religious beliefs respectively. Up to this time, he has never experienced a struggle between the two; they have coincided and reënforced one another. Now he has to make a choice between competing moral loyalties and convictions. The struggle is not between a good which is clear to him and something else which attracts him but which he knows to be wrong. It is between values each of which is an undoubted good in its place but which now get in each other's way. He is forced to reflect in order to come to a decision. Moral theory is a generalized extension of the kind of thinking in which he now engages.

There are periods in history when a whole community or a group in a community finds itself in the presence of new issues which its old customs do not adequately meet. The habits and beliefs which were formed in the past do not fit into the opportunities and requirements of contemporary life. The age in Greece following the time of Pericles was of this sort; that of the Jews af.ei their captivity; that following the Middle Ages when secular interests on a large scale were introduced into previous religious and ecclesiastic interests; the present is preëminently a period of this sort with the vast social changes which have followed the industrial expansion of the machine age.

Realization that the need for reflective morality and for moral theories grows out of conflict between ends, responsibilities, rights, and duties defines the service which moral theory may render, and also protects the student from false conceptions of its nature. The difference between customary and reflective morality is precisely that definite precepts, rules, definitive injunctions and prohibitions issue from the former, while they cannot proceed from the latter. Confusion ensues when appeal to rational principles is treated as if it were merely a substitute for custom, transferring the authority of moral commands from one source to another. Moral theory can (i) generalize the types of moral conflicts which arise, thus enabling a perplexed and doubtful individual to clarify his own particular problem by placing it in a larger context; it can (ii) state the leading ways in which such problems have been intellectually dealt with by those who have thought upon such matters; it can (iii) render personal reflection more systematic and enlightened, suggesting alternatives that might otherwise be overlooked, and stimulating greater consistency in judgment. But it does not offer a table of commandments in a catechism in which answers are as definite as are the questions which are asked. It can render personal choice more intelligent, but it cannot take the place of personal decision, which must be made in every case of moral perplexity. Such at least is the standpoint of the discussions which follow; the student who expects more from moral theory will be disappointed. The conclusion follows from the very nature of reflective morality; the attempt to set up ready-made conclusions contradicts the very nature of reflective morality.

§ 2. THE NATURE OF A MORAL ACT

Since the change from customary to reflective morality shifts emphasis from conformity to prevailing modes of action over to personal disposition and attitudes, the first business of moral theory is to obtain in outline an idea of the factors which constitute personal disposition. In its general features, the traits of a reflective moral situation have long been clear; doubts and disputes arise chiefly as to the relation which they bear to one another. The formula was well stated by Aristotle. The doer of the moral deed must have a certain "state of mind" in doing it. First, he must *know* what he is doing; secondly, he must *choose* it, and choose it for itself, and thirdly, the act must be the expression of a formed and stable *character*. In other words, the act must be *voluntary;* that is, it must manifest a choice, and for full morality at least, the choice must be an expression of the general tenor and set of personality. It must involve awareness of what one is about; a fact which in the concrete signifies that there must be a purpose, an aim, an end in view, something for the sake of which the particular act is done. The acts of infants, imbeciles, insane persons in some cases, have no moral quality; they do not know what they are about. Children learn early in life to appeal to accident, that is, absence of intention and purpose on their part, as an excuse for deeds that have bad consequences. When they exculpate themselves on the ground that they did not "mean" to do something they show a realization that intent is a normal

A.) must Br voluntary
B.) MEANS - END & intent
make a situation moral

part of a moral situation. Again, there is no choice, no implication of personal disposition, when one is coerced by superior physical power. Even when force takes the form of threats, rather than of immediate exercise of it, "duress" is at least a mitigating circumstance. It is recognized that fear of extreme harm to life and limb will overpower choice in all but those of heroic make-up.

An act must be the expression of a formed and stable character. But stability of character is an affair of degrees, and is not to be taken absolutely. No human being, however mature, has a completely formed character, while any child in the degree in which he has acquired attitudes and habits has a stable character to that extent. The point of including this qualification is that it suggests a kind of running scale of acts, some of which proceed from greater depths of the self, while others are more casual, more due to accidental and variable circumstances. We overlook acts performed under conditions of great stress or of physical weakness on the ground that the doer was "not himself" at the time. Yet we should not overdo this interpretation. Conduct may be eccentric and erratic just because a person in the past has formed that kind of disposition. An unstable character may be the product of acts deliberately chosen aforetime. A man is not himself in a state of intoxication. But a difference will be made between the case in which a usually temperate man is overcome by drink, and the case in which intoxication is so habitual as to be a sign of a habit formed by choice and of character.

May acts be voluntary, that is, be expressions of desire, intent, choice, and habitual disposition, and yet be morally neutral, indifferent? To all appearances the answer must be in the affirmative. We rise in the morning, dress, eat, and go about our usual business without attaching moral significance to what we are doing. These are the regular and normal things to do, and the acts, while many of them are performed intentionally and with a knowledge of what we are doing are a matter of course. So with the student's, merchant's, engineer's, lawyer's, or doctor's daily round of affairs. We feel that it would be rather morbid if a moral issue were raised in connection with each act; we should probably suspect some mental disorder if it were, at least some weakness in power of decision. On the other hand, we speak of the persons in question going about their daily round of *duties*. If we omitted from our estimate of moral character all the deeds done in the performance of daily tasks, satisfaction of recurrent needs, meeting of responsibilities, each slight perhaps in itself but enormous in mass, morality would be a weak and sickly thing indeed.

The inconsistency between these two points of view is only apparent. Many acts are done not only without thought of their *moral* quality but with practically no thought of any kind. Yet these acts are preconditions of other acts having significant value. A criminal on his way to commit a crime and a benevolent person on his way to a deed of mercy both have to walk or ride. Such acts, non-moral in isolation, derive moral significance from the ends to which they lead. If a man who had an important engagement to keep declined to get out of bed in the morning from sheer laziness, the indirect moral quality of a seemingly automatic act would be apparent. A vast number of acts are performed which seem to be trivial in themselves but which in reality are the supports and buttresses of acts in which definite moral considerations are present. The person who completely ignored the connection of the great number of more or less routine acts with the small number in which there is a clear moral issue would be an utterly independable person.

§ 3. CONDUCT AND CHARACTER

These facts are implicitly recognized in common speech by the use of the word *conduct*. The word expresses continuity of action, an idea which we have already met in the conception of a stable and formed character. Where there is conduct there is not simply a succession of disconnected acts but each thing done carries forward an underlying tendency and intent, *conducting*, leading up, to further acts and to a final fulfillment or consummation. Moral development, in the training given by others and in the education one secures for oneself, consists in becoming aware that our acts are connected with one another; thereby an ideal of *conduct* is substituted for the blind and thoughtless performance of isolated acts. Even when a person has attained a certain degree of moral stability, his temptations usually take the form of fancying that this particular act will not count, that it is an exception, that for this just one occasion it will not do any harm. His "temptation" is to disregard that continuity of sequence in which one act leads on to others and to a cumulative result.

We commence life under the influence of appetites and impulses, and of direct response to immediate stimuli of heat and cold, comfort and pain, light, noise, etc. The hungry child snatches at food. To him the act is innocent and natural. But he brings down reproach upon himself; he is told that he is unmannerly, inconsiderate, greedy; that he should wait till he is served, till his turn comes. He is made aware that his act has other connections than the one he had assigned to it: the immediate satisfaction of hunger. He learns to look at single acts not as single but as related links in a chain. Thus the idea of a *series*, an idea which is the essence of conduct, gradually takes the place of a mere succession of disconnected acts.

This idea of conduct as a serial whole solves the problem of morally indifferent acts. Every act has *potential* moral significance, because it is, through its consequences, part of a larger whole of behavior. A person starts to open a window because he feels the need of air—no act could be more "natural." more morally indifferent in appearance. But he remembers that his associate is an invalid and sensitive to drafts. He now sees his act in two different lights, possessed of two different values, and he has to make a choice. The potential moral import of a seemingly insignificant act has come home to him. Or, wishing to take exercise, there are two routes open to him. Ordinarily it would be a mere matter of personal taste which he would choose. But he recalls that the more pleasing of the two is longer, and that if he went that way he might be unable to keep an appointment of importance. He now has to place his act in a larger context of continuity and determine which ulterior consequence he prizes most: personal pleasure or meeting the needs of another. Thus while there is no single act which *must* under all circumstances have conscious moral quality, there is no act, since it is a part of conduct, which *may* not have definitive moral significance. There is no hard and fast line between the moraliy indifferent and the morally significant. Matthew Arnold expressed a prevailing idea when he said that conduct—in the moral sense—is three-fourths of life. Although he probably assigned it a higher ratio than most persons would, the statement expresses a widely shared idea, namely, that morality has to do with a clearly marked out portion of our life, leaving other things indifferent. Our conclusion is different. It is that *potentially* conduct is one hundred per cent of our conscious life. For all acts are so tied together that any one of them may have to be judged as an expression of character. On the other hand, there is no act which may not, under some circumstances, be morally indifferent, for at the time there may be no need for consideration of its relation to character. There is no better evidence of a well formed moral character than knowledge of when to raise the moral issue and when not. It implies a sensitiveness to values which is the token of a balanced personality. Undoubtedly many persons are so callous or so careless that they do not raise the moral issue often enough. But there are others so unbalanced that they hamper and paralyze conduct by indulging in what approaches a mania of doubt.

It is not enough to show that the binding together of acts so that they lead up to and carry one another forward constitutes conduct. We have also to consider why and how it is that they are thus bound together into a whole, instead of forming, as in the case of physical events, a mere succession. The answer is contained in rendering explicit the allusions which have been made to disposition and character. If an act were connected with other acts merely in the way in which the flame of a match is connected with an explosion of gunpowder, there would be action, but not conduct. But our actions not only lead up to other actions which follow as their effects but they also leave an enduring impress on the one who performs them, strengthening and weakening permanent tendencies to act. This fact is familiar to us in the existence of *habit*.

We are, however, likely to have a conception of habit which needs to be deepened and extended. For we are given to thinking of a habit as simply a recurrent external mode of action, like smoking or swearing, being neat or negligent in clothes and person, taking exercise, or playing games. But habit reaches even more significantly down into the very structure of the self; it signifies a building up and solidifying of certain desires; an increased sensitiveness and responsiveness to certain stimuli, a confirmed or an impaired capacity to attend to and think about certain things. Habit covers in other words the very make-up of desire, intent, choice, disposition which gives an act its voluntary quality. And this aspect of habit is much more important than that which is suggested merely by the tendency to repeated outer action, for the significance of the latter lies in the permanence of the personal disposition which is the real cause of the outer acts and of their resemblance to one another. Acts are not linked up together to form conduct in and of themselves, but because

of their common relation to an enduring and single condition—
the self or character as the abiding unity in which different
acts leave their lasting traces. If one surrenders to a momentary impulse, the significant thing is not the particular
act which follows, but the strengthening of the power of that
impulse—this strengthening is the reality of that which we
call habit. In giving way, the person in so far commits himself
not just to *that* isolated act but to a *course* of action, to a *line*
of behavior.

Sometimes a juncture is so critical that a person, in deciding
upon what course he will take, feels that his future, his very
being, is at stake. Such cases are obviously of great practical
importance for the person concerned. They are of importance
for theory, because some degree of what is conspicuous in
these momentous cases is found in *every* voluntary decision.
Indeed, also it belongs to acts performed impulsively without
deliberate choice. In such cases, it is later experience which
makes us aware of the serious commitment implied in an earlier
act. We find ourselves involved in embarrassing complications
and on reflection we trace the cause of our embarrassment to a
deed which we performed casually, without reflection and
deliberate intent. Then we reflect upon the value of the entire class of actions. We realize the difference which exists
between the thought of an act before it is done and as it is
experienced afterwards. As Goldsmith so truly said "In the
first place, we cook the dish to our own appetite; in the latter,
nature cooks it for us." We plunge at first into action pushed
by impulse, drawn by appetite. After we have acted and
consequences which are unexpected and undesired show themselves, we begin to reflect. We review the wisdom or the
rightness of the course which we engaged in with little or no
thought. Our judgment turns backward for its material;
something has turned out differently than we anticipated,
and so we think back to discover what was the matter. But
while the material of the judgment comes to us from the

past, what really concerns us is what we shall do the next time; the function of reflection is prospective. We wish to decide whether to continue in the course of action entered upon or to shift to another. The person who reflects on his past action in order to get light on his future behavior is the conscientious person. There is always a temptation to seek for something external to the self on which to lay the blame when things go wrong; we dislike to trace the cause back to something in ourselves. When this temptation is yielded to, a person becomes irresponsible; he neither pins himself nor can be pinned down by others to any consistent course of action, for he will not institute any connection of cause and effect between his character and his deeds.

The conclusion is that conduct and character are strictly correlative. Continuity, consistency, throughout a series of acts is the expression of the enduring unity of attitudes and habits. Deeds hang together because they proceed from a single and stable self. Customary morality tends to neglect or blur the connection between character and action; the essence of reflective morals is that it is conscious of the existence of a persistent self and of the part it plays in what is externally done. Leslie Stephen has expressed this principle as follows:

"The clear enunciation of one principle seems to be a characteristic of all great moral revolutions. The recognition amounts almost to a discovery, and may be said to mark the point at which the *moral* code first becomes distinctly separated from other codes. It may be briefly expressed in the phrase that morality is internal. The *moral* law, we may say, has to be expressed in the form, "be this," not in the form, "do this." The possibility of expressing any rule in this form may be regarded as deciding whether it can or cannot have a distinctively moral character. Christianity gave prominence to the doctrine that the true moral law says "hate not," instead of "kill not." The men of old time had forbidden adultery: the new moral teacher forbade lust; and his greatness as a moral teacher was manifested in nothing more than in the clearness with which he gave utterance to this doctrine. It would

person (self) and
actions (character/conduct)
are not separate
but self is amalgamated

be easy to show how profoundly the same doctrine, in various forms, has been bound up with other moral and religious reformations in many ages of the world." [1]

§ 4. MOTIVE AND CONSEQUENCES

In reaching the conclusion that conduct and character are morally one and the same thing, first taken as effect and then as causal and productive factor, we have virtually disposed of one outstanding point of controversy in moral theory. The issue in question is that between those who hold that *motives* are the only thing which count morally and those who hold that *consequences* are alone of moral import. On one side stand those who, like Kant, say that results actually attained are of no importance morally speaking, because they do not depend upon the will alone; that only the will can be good or bad in the moral sense. On the other side, are those who, like Bentham, say that morality consists in producing consequences which contribute to the general welfare, and that motives do not count at all save as they happen to influence the consequences one way or another. One theory puts sole emphasis upon *attitude*, upon *how* the chosen act is conceived and inspired; the other theory lays stress solely upon *what* is actually done, upon the objective *content* of the deed in the way of its effect upon others. Our analysis shows that both views are one-sided. At whichever end we begin we find ourselves intellectually compelled to consider the other end. We are dealing not with two different things but with two poles of the same thing. The school of Bentham, for example, does not hold that *every* consequence is of importance in judging an act morally. It would not say that the act of a surgeon is necessarily to be condemned because an operation results in the death of a patient. It limits the theory to *foreseen* and desired consequences. The intended consequence, the intention, of the surgeon was to save life; morally his act was beneficent,

[1] *Science of Ethics*, p. 155.

although unsuccessful from causes which he could not control. They say if his *intent* was right, it makes no difference what his *motive* was; whether he was moved by kindly feeling, by desire for professional standing, by a wish to show his skill, or to gain a fee, is immaterial. The only thing that counts morally is that he intended to effect certain consequences.

The protest contained in this position against locating morals in the conscious feeling which attends the doing of an act is valuable and valid. Persons, children and grown-ups alike, often say in justification for some act that turned out badly that they meant well; they allege some innocent or amiable feeling as the "motive" of the act. The real fact in all probability was that they took next to no pains to think out the consequences of what they proposed to do. They kept their minds upon any favorable results that might be fancied to follow, and glossed over or kept from view its undesirable consequences. If "motive" signified the emotional state which happens to exist in consciousness at the time of acting, Bentham's position would be entirely sound. Since that conception of motives is more or less prevalent, he was not setting up a man of straw to hit, but was attacking a doctrine which is morally dangerous. For it encourages men to neglect the purpose and bearing of their actions, and to justify what they feel inclined to do on the ground that their feelings when doing it were innocent and amiable.

The underlying identification of motive with personal feeling is, however, erroneous. What moves a man is not a feeling but the set disposition, of which a feeling is at best but a dubious indication. An emotion, as the word suggests, moves us, but an emotion is a good deal more than a bare "feeling"; anger is not so much a state of conscious feeling as it is a tendency to act in a destructive way towards whatever arouses it. It is doubtful if a miserly person is conscious of feelings of stinginess; he rather prizes that which he hoards and is moved to keep up and conserve that which he prizes. Just as an angry person may deny, quite honestly, that he is angry, so an ambitious man is likely to be quite devoid of any *feeling* of ambition. There are objects and ends which arouse his energy and into the attaining of which he throws himself with whole-heartedness. If he were to interpret his own conduct he would say that he acts as he does not because of personal ambition, but because the objects in question are so important.

When it is recognized that "motive" is but an abbreviated name for the attitude and predisposition toward ends which is embodied in action, all ground for making a sharp separation between motive and intention—foresight of consequences—falls away. Mere foresight of results may be coldly intellectual, like a prediction of an eclipse. It moves to action only when it is accompanied with desire for that sort of result. On the other hand, a set and disposition of character leads to anticipation of certain kinds of consequences and to passing over other effects of action without notice. A careless man will not be aware of consequences that occur to a prudent man; if they do present themselves to thought, he will not attach the force to them which the careful man does. A crafty character will foresee consequences which will not occur to a frank and open man; if they should happen to come to the mind of the latter, he will be repelled by the very considerations that would attract the sly and intriguing person. Othello and Iago foresee different consequences because they have different kinds of characters. Thus the formation of intention, of purpose, is a function of the forces of human nature which lead to action, and the foreseen consequences move to action only as they are also prized and desired. The distinction between motive and intent is not found in the facts themselves, but is simply a result of our own analysis, according as we emphasize either the emotional or the intellectual aspect of an action. The theoretical value of the utilitarian position consists in the fact that it warns us against overlooking the essential place of the intellectual factor, namely, foresight of consequences. The practical value of the theory which lays stress on motive is that it calls attention to the part played by character, by personal disposition and attitude, in determining the direction which the intellectual factor takes.

But in its extreme form it suffers from the same one-sidedness as does the Benthamite theory of intention, although in the opposite direction. It is possible to make good sense of the proposition that it is the "will" which counts morally, rather than consequences. But only so, if we recognize that *will* signifies an active tendency to foresee consequences, to form resolute purposes, and to use all the efforts at command to produce the intended consequences in fact. The idea that consequences are morally irrelevant is true only in the sense that any act is always likely to have some consequences which could not have been foreseen, even with the best will in the world. We always build better or worse than we know, and the best laid plans of men as of mice are more or less at the mercy of uncontrollable contingent circumstances when it comes to actual consequences. But this fact of the limitation of intention cannot be converted into the doctrine that there is such a thing as motive and will apart from projection of consequences and from effort to bring them to pass. "Will," in the sense of unity of impulse, desire, and thought which anticipates and plans, is central in morals just because by its very nature it is the most constant and effectual factor in control of consequences.

This emphasis upon character is not peculiar to any special type of moral theory. Our dominating interest is the manifestation and interaction of personalities. It is the same interest which shows itself in the drama where the colorful display of incidents is, save in the melodramatic and sentimental, a display of the outworking of character. Political thought tends to be too much rather than too little concerned with personality at the expense of issues and principles. What Hamlet, Macbeth, Nora, Tartuffe are to the theater, Roosevelt,

Wilson, Lloyd George, Mussolini are to politics. For practical reasons we must be concerned with character in our daily affairs. Whether we buy or sell goods, lend money or invest in securities, call a physician or consult a lawyer, take or refuse advice from a friend, fall in love and marry, the ultimate outcome depends upon the characters which are involved.

§ 5. PRESENT NEED OF THEORY

We have already noted in passing that the present time is one which is in peculiar need of reflective morals and of a working theory of morals. The scientific outlook on the world and on life has undergone and is still undergoing radical change. Methods of industry, of the production, and distribution of goods have been completely transformed. The basic conditions on which men meet and associate, in work and amusement, have been altered. There has been a vast dislocation of older habits and traditions. Travel and migration are as common as they were once unusual. The masses are educated enough to read and a prolific press exists which supplies cheap reading matter. Schooling has ceased to be the privilege of the few and has become the right and even the enforced duty of the many. The stratification of society into classes each fairly homogeneous in itself has been broken into. The area of contacts with persons and populations alien to our bringing up and traditions has enormously extended. A ward of a large city in the United States may have persons of from a score to fifty racial origins. The walls and barriers that once separated nations have become less important because of the railway, steamship, telegraph, telephone, and radio.

Only a few of the more obvious changes in social conditions and interests have been mentioned. Each one of them has created new problems and issues that contain moral values which are uncertain and disputed. Nationalism and internationalism, capital and labor, war and peace, science and religious tradition, competition and coöperation, *laissez faire* and State planning in industry, democracy and dictatorship in government, rural and city life, personal work and control *versus* investment and vicarious riches through stocks and bonds, native born and alien, contact of Jew and Gentile, of white and colored, of Catholic and Protestant, and those of new religions: a multitude of such relationships have brought to the fore new moral problems with which neither old customs nor beliefs are competent to cope. In addition, the rapidity with which social changes occur brings moral unsettlement and tends to destroy many ties which were the chief safeguards of the morals of custom. There was never a time in the history of the world when human relationships and their accompanying rights and duties, opportunities and demands, needed the unremitting and systematic attention of intelligent thought as they do at present.

There are those who tend to minimize the importance of reflection in moral issues. They hold that men already know more morally than they practice and that there is general agreement among men on all moral fundamentals. Usually such persons will be found to adhere to some especial tradition in whose dogmas they find final and complete authority. But in fact the agreement exists to a large extent only with reference to concepts that are taken vaguely and apart from practical application. Justice: to be sure; give to each that which is his due. But is individualistic competitive capitalism a just system? or socialism? or communism? Is inheritance of large fortunes, without rendering of personal service to society, just? What system of taxation is just? What are the moral claims of free-trade and protection? What would constitute a just system of the distribution of national income? Few would question the desirability of chastity, but there are a multitude of interpretations of its meaning. Does it mean that celibacy is more pleasing to God than marriage? This idea is not generally held today, but its former vogue still affects the beliefs and practices of men and women. What is the relation of

chastity as a moral idea to divorce, birth control, state censorship of literature? Human life is sacred. But what about many
of the health-destroying practices and accident-inducing practices of modern industry? What about war, preparation for
which absorbs the chief part of the revenue of modern States?

And so we could go down the list of all the time-honored
virtues and duties, and show that changes in conditions have
made what they signify for human action a matter of uncer-
tainty and controversy. The ultimate difference, for example,
between the employing and the employed in industry is one
of moral criteria and outlook. They envisage different values
as having a superior claim. The same is evidently even more
true of the convinced nationalist and internationalist, pacifist
and militarist, secularist and devotee of authoritatively revealed religion. Now it is not held for a moment that moral
theory can give direct and final answers to these questions.
But it is held that they cannot be dealt with by adherence to
mere tradition nor by trusting to casual impulse and momentary inspiration. Even if all men agreed sincerely to act upon
the principle of the Golden Rule as the supreme law of conduct,
we should still need inquiry and thought to arrive at even a
passable conception of what the Rule means in terms of concrete practice under mixed and changing social conditions.
Universal agreement upon the abstract principle even if it
existed would be of value only as a preliminary to coöperative
undertaking of investigation and thoughtful planning; as a
preparation, in other words, for systematic and consistent
reflection.

§ 6. SOURCES OF MORAL THEORY

No theory can operate in a vacuum. Moral as well as physical theory requires a body of dependable data, and a set of
intelligible working hypotheses. Where shall moral theory
find the material with which to satisfy these needs?

1. While all that has been said about the extent of change

in all conditions of life is true, nevertheless there has been no complete breach of continuity. From the beginning of human life, men have arrived at some conclusions regarding what is proper and fair in human relationships, and have engaged in working out codes of conduct. The dogmatist, whether made so by tradition or through some special insight which he claims as his own, will pick out from the many conflicting codes that one which agrees the most closely with his own education and taste. A genuinely reflective morals will look upon all the codes as possible *data;* it will consider the conditions under which they arose; the methods which consciously or unconsciously determined their formation and acceptance; it will inquire into their applicability in present conditions. It will neither insist dogmatically upon some of them, nor idly throw them all away as of no significance. It will treat them as a storehouse of information and possible indications of what is now right and good.

2. Closely connected with this body of material in codes and convictions, is the more consciously elaborated material of legal history, judicial decisions, and legislative activity. Here we have a long experimentation in working out principles for direction of human beings in their conduct. Something of the same kind is true of the workings of all great human institutions. The history of the family, of industry, of property systems, of government and the state, of education and art, is full of instructions about modes of human conduct and the consequences of adopting this or that mode of conduct. Informal material of the same sort abounds in biographies, especially of those who have been selected as the great moral teachers of the race.

3. A resource which mankind was late in utilizing and which it has hardly as yet begun to draw upon adequately is found in the various sciences, especially those closest to man, such as biology, physiology, hygiene and medicine, psychology and psychiatry, as well as statistics, sociology, economics, and

politics. The latter upon the whole present problems rathei
than solutions. But it is well to get problems more clearly iu
mind, and the very fact that these social disciplines usually
approach their material independently of consideration of
moral values has a certain intellectual advantage for the
moralist. For although he still has to translate economic and
political statement over into moral terms, there is some guarantee of intellectual objectivity and impartiality in the fact
that these sciences approach their subject-matter in greater
detachment from preformed and set moral convictions, since
the latter may be only the prejudices of tradition or temperament. From the biological and psychological sciences, there are
derivable highly valuable techniques for study of human and
social problems and the opening of new vistas. For example,
the discovery of the conditions and the consequences of health
of body, personal and public, which these sciences have already
effected, opens the way to a relatively new body of moral
interests and responsibilities. It is impossible any longer to
regard health and the conditions which affect it as a merely
technical or physical matter. Its ramifications with moral
order and disorder have been clearly demonstrated.

4. Then there is the body of definitely theoretical methods
and conclusions which characterize European history for the
last two thousand years, to say nothing of the doctrines of
Asiatic thinkers for a still longer period. Keen intellects
have been engaged in analysis and in the development of directive principles on a rational basis. Alternative positions
and their implications have been explored and systematically
developed. At first sight, the variety of logically incompatible
positions which have been taken by theorists may seem to the
student to indicate simply a scene of confusion and conflict.
But when studied more closely they reveal the complexity of
moral situations, a complexity so great that while every theory
may be found to ignore factors and relations which ought to be
taken into account, each one will also be found to bring to

light some phase of the moral life demanding reflective attention, and which, save for it, might have remained hidden. The
proper inference to be drawn is not that we should make a
mechanical compromise or an eclectic combination of the
different theories, but that each great system of moral thought
brings to light some point of view from which the facts of our
own situations are to be looked at and studied. Theories
afford us at least a set of questions with which we may approach and challenge present conditions.

§ 7. CLASSIFICATION OF PROBLEMS

For the remaining portion of this Second Part we shall be
occupied mainly with a consideration of some of the chief
classic theories about morals which have left a moral impress
on civilization. A survey of these theories brings out certain
underlying differences of emphasis and resulting intellectual
problems, which the student will be put in possession of,
before taking up the conceptions themselves. Roughly speaking, theories will be found to vary primarily because some of
them attach chief importance to purposes and ends, leading
to the concept of the *Good* as ultimate; while some others
are impressed by the importance of law and regulation,
leading up to the supremacy of the concepts of *Duty* and the
Right; while a third set regards approbation and disapprobation, praise and blame as the primary moral fact, thus termi-
nating with making the concepts of *Virtue* and *Vice* central.
Within each tendency, there are further differences of opinion
as to what is the Good, the nature of Duty, Law, and the
Right, and the relative standing of different virtues.

1. That men form purposes, strive for the realization of
ends, is an established fact. If it is asked why they do so, the
only answer to the question, aside from saying that they do
so unreasonably from mere blind custom, is that they strive
to attain certain goals because they believe that these ends
have an intrinsic value of their own; they are *good*, satisfactory.

The chief province of reason in practical matters is to discriminate between ends that merely seem good and those which
are really so—between specious, deceptive goods, and lasting
true goods. Men have desires; immediately and apart from
reflection they want this and that thing, food, a companion,
money, fame and repute, health, distinction among their fellows,
power, the love of friends, the admiration of rivals, etc. But
why do they want these things? Because value is attributed
to them; because they are thought to be good. As the scholas-
tics said, we desire *sub specie boni;* beneath all the special ends
striven for is the common idea of the Good, the Satisfying.
Theories which regard *ends* as the important thing in morals
accordingly make the conception of Good central in theory.
Since men often take things to be good in anticipatory judgment which are not so in fact, the problem of this group of
theories is to determine the *real* good as distinct from the
things that merely *seem* to be so, or, what is the same thing,
the permanent good from transitory and fleeting goods. From
the side of attitude and disposition, the fundamental matter
is therefore the *insight and wisdom* which is able to discriminate
between ends that deceptively promise satisfaction and the
ends which truly constitute it. The great problem of morals
on this score is the attainment of right knowledge.

2. To other observers of human life, the *control* of desire
and appetite has seemed much more fundamental than their
satisfaction. Many of them are suspicious of the very principle of desire and of the ends which are connected with it.
Desire seems to them so personal and so bent on its own satisfaction as to be the source of temptation, to be the cause which
leads men to deviate from the lawful course of action. Empirically, these thinkers are struck by the rôle played in
human government by commands, prohibitions, and all the
devices that regulate the play of passions and desires. To
them, the great problem is to discover some underlying
authority which shall control the formation of aims and pur-

poses. The lower animals follow desire and appetite because they have no conception of regulative law; men have the consciousness of being *bound* by a principle superior to impulse and want. The morally *right* and the naturally satisfying are often in conflict and the heart of the moral struggle is to subordinate good to the demands of *duty*. The theory that makes ends supreme has been called the *teleological* (from the Greek, τέλος, end); the theory which makes law and duty supreme, the *jural*.

3. There is another group of thinkers who feel that the principle of ends and rational insight places altogether too much emphasis upon the intellectual factor in human nature, and that the theory of law and duty is too legal, external, and stringent. They are struck by the enormous part played in human life by facts of approbation and condemnation, praise and blame, reward and punishment, encouragement of some courses of action, resentment at others, and pressure to keep persons from adopting those courses which are frowned upon. They find in human nature a spontaneous tendency to favor some lines of conduct, and to censure and penalize other modes of action, a tendency which in time is extended from acts to the dispositions from which the acts flow. Out of the mass of approbations arise the ideas of virtue and vice; the dispositions which are socially commended and encouraged constituting the excellencies of character which are to be cultivated, vices and defects being those traits which are condemned. Those who hold to this theory have no difficulty in demonstrating the great rôle of commendation and disfavor in customary morality. The problem of reflective morality and hence of theory is to lay bare the standard or criterion implicit in current social approbation and reproach. In general, they agree that what men like and praise are acts and motives that tend to serve others, while those acts and motives which are condemned are those which bring harm instead of benefit to others. Reflective morality makes this

principle of popular moral judgments conscious, and one to be *rationally* adopted and exercised.

In our succeeding chapters we shall consider these three types of theory and the various subdivisions into which they have evolved. Our aim will be not so much to determine which is true and which false as to see what factors of permanent value each group contributes to the clarification and direction of reflective morality.

LITERATURE

See Sharp, *Ethics*, 1928, ch. i.; Martineau, *Types of Ethical Theory*, 1891, Vol. I., Introduction; Sorley, *Recent Tendencies in Ethics*, 1904; Moore, *Philo, sophical Studies*, 1922, essay on "The Nature of Moral Philosophy"; Broad, *Five Types of Ethical Theory*, 1930; Fite, *Moral Philosophy*, 1925, ch. i.; James-"The Moral Philosopher and the Moral Life," in *The Will to Believe*, 1912, Otto, *Things and Ideals*, 1924, ch. v.; Levy-Bruhl, *Ethics and Moral Science*; trans. 1905; Everett, *Moral Values*, 1918, ch. i.

On CONDUCT AND CHARACTER in general, see Paulsen, *System of Ethics*, 1899, pp. 468–472; Mackenzie, *Manual of Ethics*, 1901, Book I., ch. iii.; Spencer, *Principles of Ethics*, Part I., chs. ii.–viii.; Green, *Prolegomena to Ethics*, 1890, pp. 110–117, 152–159; Alexander, *Moral Order and Progress*, pp. 48–52; Stephen, *Science of Ethics*, 1882, ch. ii.; Mezes, *Ethics*, 1901, ch. iv.; Seth, *Ethical Principles*, 1898, ch. iii.; Dewey, *Human Nature and Conduct*, 1922.

Upon MOTIVE AND INTENTION consult Bentham, *Principles of Morals and Legislation*, chs. viii. and x.; Mill, *Analysis of Human Mind*, Vol. II., chs. xxii., and xxv.; Austin, *Jurisprudence*, Vol. I., chs. viii.–xx.; Green, *Prolegomena*, 1890, pp. 315–325; Alexander, *Moral Order and Progress*, pp. 36–47; Westermarck, *Origin and Development of the Moral Ideas*, 1906, chs. viii., xi., and xiii.; Ritchie, *International Journal of Ethics*, Vol. IV., pp. 89–94, and 229–238, where further references are given; Dewey, *Human Nature and Conduct*, 1922, pp. 118–122.

CHAPTER II

ENDS, THE GOOD AND WISDOM

§ 1. REFLECTION AND ENDS

THE question of what ends a man should live for does not arise as a general problem in customary morality. It is forestalled by the habits and institutions which a person finds existing all about him. What others, especially elders, are doing provides the ends for which one should act. These ends are sanctioned by tradition; they are hallowed by the semidivine character of the ancestors who instituted the customs; they are set forth by the wise elders, and are enforced by the rulers. Individuals trespass, deviating from these established purposes, but they do so with the conviction that thereby social condemnation, reënforced by supernatural penalties inflicted by divine beings, ensues. There are today multitudes of men and women who take their aims from what they observe to be going on around them. They accept the aims provided by religious teachers, by political authorities, by persons in the community who have prestige. Failure to adopt such a course would seem to many persons to be a kind of moral rebellion or anarchy. Many other persons find their ends practically forced upon them. Because of lack of education and because of economic stress they for the most part do just what they have to do. In the absence of the possibility of real choice, such a thing as reflection upon purposes and the attempt to frame a general theory of ends and of the good would seem to be idle luxuries.

There can, however, be no such thing as reflective morality except where men seriously ask by what purposes they should direct their conduct and why they should do so: what it is

29

which makes their purposes good. This intellectual search for ends is bound to arise when customs fail to give required guidance. And this failure happens when old institutions break down; when invasions from without and inventions and innovations from within radically alter the course of life.

If habit fails, the sole alternative to caprice and random action is reflection. And reflection upon what one shall do is identical with formation of ends. Moreover, when social change is great, and a great variety of conflicting aims are suggested, reflection cannot be limited to the selection of one end out of a number which are suggested by conditions. Thinking has to operate creatively to form new ends.

Every habit introduces continuity into activity; it furnishes a permanent thread or axis. When custom breaks down, the only thing which can link together the succession of various acts is a common purpose running through separate acts. An end-in-view gives unity and continuity, whether it be the securing of an education, the carrying on of a military campaign, or the building of a house. ¡The more inclusive the aim in question the broader is the unification which is attained. Comprehensive ends may connect together acts performed during a long span of years. To the common soldier or even to the general in command, winning the campaign may be a sufficiently comprehensive aim to unify acts into conduct. But some one is bound to ask: What then? To what uses shall victory when achieved be put? At least that question is bound to be asked, provided men are intelligently interested in their behavior and are not governed by chance and the pressure of the passing moment. *The development of inclusive and enduring aims is the necessary condition of the application of reflection in conduct; indeed, they are two names for the same fact.* There can be no such thing as reflective morality where there is not solicitude for the ends to which action is directed.

Habit and impulse have consequences, just as every occurrence has effects. But merely as habit, impulse, and appetite they do not lead to foresight of what will happen as a consequence of their operation. An animal is moved by hunger and the outcome is satisfaction of appetite and the nourishment of the body. In the case of a human being, having mature experience upon which to fall back, obstacles in the way of satisfaction of hunger, difficulties encountered in the pursuit of food, will make a man aware of *what* he wants:—the outcome will be anticipated as an end-in-view, as something desired and striven for. Behavior has ends in the sense of results which *put an end* to that particular activity, while an *end-in-view* arises when a particular consequence is foreseen and being foreseen is consciously adopted by desire and deliberately made the directive purpose of action. A purpose or aim represents a craving, an urge, translated into the idea of an object, as blind hunger is transformed into a purpose through the thought of a food which is wanted, say flour, which then develops into the thought of grain to be sown and land to be cultivated:—a whole series of activities to be intelligently carried on.

An end-in-view thus differs on one side from a mere anticipation or prediction of an outcome, and on the other side from the propulsive force of mere habit and appetite. In distinction from the first, it involves a want, an impulsive urge and forward drive; in distinction from the second, it involves an intellectual factor, the thought of an object which gives meaning and direction to the urge. This connection between purpose and desire is the source of one whole class of moral problems. Attainment of learning, professional skill, wealth, power, would not be animating purposes unless the thought of some result were unified with some intense need of the self, for it takes *thought* to convert an impulse into a desire centered in an object. But on the other end, a strong craving tends to exclude thought. It is in haste for its own speedy realization. An intense appetite, say thirst, impels to immediate action without thought of its consequences, as a very thirsty

man at sea tends to drink salt water without regard to objective results. Deliberation and inquiry, on the other hand, take
time; they demand delay, the deferring of immediate action.
Craving does not look beyond the moment, but it is of the
very nature of thought to look toward a remote end.

§ 2. ENDS AND THE GOOD: THE UNION OF DESIRE AND THOUGHT

There is accordingly a conflict brought about within the
self. The impetus of reflection when it is aroused is to look
ahead; to hunt out and to give weight to remoter consequences.
But the force of craving, the impulsion of immediate need,
call thought back to some near-by object in which want will
find its immediate and direct satisfaction. The wavering and
conflict which result are the ground for the theory which holds
that there is an inherent warfare in the moral life between
desire and reason; the theory that appetite and desire tend to
delude us with deceptive goods, leading us away from the true
end that reason holds up to view. In consequence, some moralists have gone so far as to hold that appetite and impulse
are inherently evil, being expressions of the lust of the flesh,
a power which pulls men away from the ends which reason
approves. This view, however, is impossible. No idea or
object could operate as an end and become a purpose unless
it were connected with some need; otherwise it would be a mere
idea without any moving and impelling power.

In short, while there is conflict, it is not between desire and
reason, but between a desire which wants a near-by object
and a desire which wants an object which is seen by thought
to occur in consequence of an intervening series of conditions,
or in the "long run"; it is a conflict between two objects presented in thought, one corresponding to a want or appetite
just as it presents itself in isolation, the other corresponding to the want thought of in relation to other wants. Fear
may suggest flight or lying to a man as ends to be sought;
further thought may bring a man to a conviction that

steadfastness and truthfulness will insure a much larger and more enduring good. There is an idea in each case; in the first case, an idea of personal safety; in the second instance, an idea of, say, the safety of others to be achieved by remaining at a post. In each case also there is desire; in the first instance a desire which lies close to natural impulse and instinct; in the second instance, a desire which would not be aroused were it not that *thought* brings into view remote consequences. *In one case, original impulse dictates the thought of the object; in the other case, this original impulse is transformed into a different desire because of objects which thought holds up to view.* But no matter how elaborate and how rational is the object of thought, it is impotent unless it arouses desire.

In other words, there is nothing intrinsically bad about raw impulse and desire. They *become* evil in contrast with another desire whose object includes more inclusive and more enduring consequences. What is morally dangerous in the desire as it first shows itself is its tendency to confine attention to its own immediate object and to shut out the thought of a larger whole of conduct.

William James has truly described the situation.

"What constitutes the difficulty for a man laboring under an unwise passion to act as if the passion were unwise? . . . The difficulty is mental; it is that of getting the idea of the wise action to stay before the mind at all. Whenever any strong emotional state is upon us, the tendency is for no images but those which are congruous with it to come up. If others by chance offer themselves, they are instantly smothered and crowded out. . . . By a sort of self-preserving instinct which our passion has, it feels that these chill objects if they once but gain a lodgment will work and work till they have frozen the very vital spark from out of all our mood. Passion's cue accordingly is always and everywhere to prevent the still small voice from being heard at all." [1]

[1] *Principles of Psychology*, Vol. II., pp. 562–563. The entire passage, pp. 561–569, should be consulted. What is said Vol. 1., pp. 284–290, on the selective operation of feeling should also be consulted.

The conclusion that the conflict is not between impulse and want on the one hand, and a rational end on the other, but between two desires and two ends present in thought, agrees with our practical experience. Sometimes persons who have been subjected to one-sided moral training feel shame and remorse because some malicious or foul idea has come into their minds, even though they have not acted upon it but have speedily dismissed it. Momentary impulses enter our minds by all sorts of channels. Unless a person is responsible for having previously cultivated habits which excite and strengthen them, he has no ground for moral blame of himself, merely because the idea of a certain end has "popped into his head." His moral condition depends upon what he does with the idea *after* it has presented itself. That is to say, the real object of moral judgment is a union between thought and purposeful desire. There is also a temptation to indulge freely in purely imaginative satisfactions of desires known to be unworthy, on the ground that no harm is done as long as the desires are kept within the realm of fancy and do not pass into overt conduct. This view of things overlooks the fact that giving way to *thoughts* of the pleasurable satisfaction of desires actually strengthens the force of a desire and adds to its power to eventuate in overt action on some future occasion. There can be no separation morally of desire and thought because the union of thought and desire is just what makes an act voluntary.

The same result is reached when we consider inhibition of desire *versus* free surrender to it. There are different kinds of inhibition, and they have very different moral values and consequences. One sort is a deliberate exclusion of the appetite and impulse from the field of thinking and observation; there is then a suppression which simply drives the desire into underground channels. In this case there is no weakening of its power, but only a shift so that it exercises its power indirectly. On the other hand, all thinking exercises by its very nature an inhibitory effect. It delays the operation of desire, and tends to call up new considerations which alter the nature of the action to which one felt originally impelled. This inhibitory action does not consist in smothering or suppressing desire but in transforming a desire into a form which is more intelligent because more cognizant of relations and bearings.

A third confirmation in practical experience is found in the issue of sacrifice *versus* indulgence. Here too we find that the true solution of the problem lies in bringing thought and desire together instead of pitting them against each other. Sometimes sacrifice is made an end in itself. This is equivalent to treating an impulse as evil in and of itself. Sacrifice of this sort ends in maiming life, curtailing power, and narrowing the horizon of opportunities for action. But there is another kind of re-nunciation which takes place when some end is perceived which is judged to be more worthy, and desire is attached to this better end which thought discloses. No one can have everything he wants; our powers are too limited and our environment too unyielding to permit of any such state of affairs. In consequence we must give up, sacrifice, some objects which desire places before us. Unwillingness to make *any* sacrifice merely indicates immaturity of character, like that of a young child who supposes he can compass all the objects of his heart's desire. Reflection has its normal func-tion in placing the objects of desire in a perspective of relative values, so that when we give up one good we do it because we see another which is of greater worth and which evokes a more inclusive and a more enduring desire. We then escape from that kind of renunciation which Goethe called blasphemous, as well as from that which makes it a good in and of itself. For as Goethe pointed out, renunciation tends to be thought-less. "We renounce particular things at each moment by sheer levity, if only we can grasp something else the next moment. We merely put one passion in place of another:

business, inclinations, amusements, hobbies. We try them all, one after another, only to cry out in the end that 'all is vanity.'" Once more, thoughtful desire is the alternative both to suppression of desire and to yielding to a desire just as it first presents itself.

An understanding of the relationship between the propulsive, urging force of desire and the widening scope of thought enables us to understand what is meant by *will*, especially by the term a "strong will." Sometimes the latter is confused with mere stiff-necked obstinacy—a blind refusal to alter one's purpose no matter what new considerations thinking can produce. Sometimes it is confused with an intense although brief display of spasmodic external energy, even though the forceful manifestation is nothing better than a great ado about nothing. In reality "strength of will" (or, to speak more advisedly, of character) consists of an abiding identification of impulse with thought, in which impulse provides the drive while thought supplies consecutiveness, patience, and persistence, leading to a unified course of conduct. It is not the same as obstinacy because instead of insisting on repetition of the same act, it is observant of changes of conditions and is flexible in making new adjustments. It is *thinking* which is persisted in, even though special ends in view change, while the obstinate person insists upon the same act even when thinking would disclose a wiser course. In the passage quoted, James says that the difficulty in holding to a resolution when a strong passion is upon us is *mental*. It consists in the difficulty of maintaining an idea, in keeping attention alert and continuous. But at the same time, *mere* thinking would not lead to action; thinking must be taken up into vital impulse and desire in order to have body and weight in action.

From the peculiar union of desire and thought in voluntary action, it follows that every moral theory which tries to determine the *end* of conduct has a double aspect. In its relation to *desire*, it requires a theory of the *Good*: the Good is that which satisfies want, craving, which fulfills or makes complete the need which stirs to action. In its relation to *thought*, or as an *idea* of an object to be attained, it imposes upon those about to act the necessity for rational insight, or moral *wisdom*. For experience shows, as we have seen, that not every satisfaction of appetite and craving turns out to be a good; many ends *seem* good while we are under the influence of strong passion which in actual experience and in such thought as might have occurred in a cool moment are actually bad. The task of moral theory is thus to frame a theory of Good as the end or objective of desire, and also to frame a theory of the true, as distinct from the specious, good. In effect this latter need signifies the discovery of ends which will meet the demands of impartial and far-sighted thought as well as satisfy the urgencies of desire.

This double aspect of ends gives a clew to the consideration of the different theories which have been advanced, and also a criterion for judging their worth. A theory may appear, superficially, to offer a conception of the Good that connects it in a satisfactory way with desire and yet fail to provide the conditions which alone would enable the end to afford intelligent direction to conduct. This is especially true of the first theory which we shall now take up.

§ 3. PLEASURE AS THE GOOD AND THE END

To many minds it has seemed not only plausible but practically self-evident that what makes any object of desire and of attainment good is the pleasure which it gives to the one who has the experience. We find mankind seeking for many and for diverse objects. But why? What is the common quality which renders all these different things desirable? According to the theory under discussion (called *Hedonism*, from the Greek ἡδονή, signifying pleasure) this common quality is pleasure. The evidence for the theory is asserted to be found in experience itself. Why does and why should any one seek for any object unless he believes it will be enjoyed? Why should any one avoid any object as evil unless he believes its experience will be painful? The words of Bain and of John Stuart Mill are typical. The former said: "There can be no proof offered for the position that happiness is the proper end of all human procedures. . . . It is an ultimate or final assumption to be tested by reference to the individual judgments of mankind." The latter said: "The only proof capable of being given that an object is visible is that people actually see it. In like manner the sole proof it is possible to produce that anything is desirable is that people do actually desire it."

Without going into detail at this point, we may anticipate the discussion which follows to the extent of saying that such statements suffer from a fatal ambiguity. Happiness may be the Good and yet happiness not be the same thing as pleasure. Again, the ending "able" has two meanings in different words. It signifies "*capable* of being seen," when it occurs in the word "visible." But in other words, it signifies that which is fit, proper, as in the words "enjoyable," "lovable." "Desirable" signifies not that which is capable of being desired (experience shows that about everything has been desired by some one at some time) but that which in the eye of impartial thought *should* be desired. It is true, of course, that it would be foolish to set up anything as the end of desire, or as desirable, which is not actually desired or capable of being desired. But it would be equally stupid to assume that what *should* be desired can be determined by a mere examination of what men do desire, until a critical examination of the *reasonableness* of things desired has taken place. So there is a distinction between the enjoy*ed* and the enjoy*able*.

We have then to examine the hedonistic theory both as a theory of desire and as a theory of practical wisdom or prudence in the choice of ends to be pursued. The very idea of an *end* implies something more or less distant, remote; it implies the need of looking ahead, of judging. The advice which it gives to desire is: *Respice finem.* Consider how you will come out if you act upon the desire you now feel; count the cost. Calculate consequences over a period of time. Circumspection, prudent estimate of the whole course of consequences set in train, is the precondition of attaining satisfaction or the Good. All folly and stupidity consist in failure to consider the remote, the long run, because of the engrossing and blinding power exercised by some present intense desire.

Our first criticism is devoted to showing that if pleasure be taken as the end, no such cool and far-seeing judgment of consequences as the theory calls for is possible; in other words, it defeats itself. For consequences in the way of pleasures and pains are just the things in the way of consequences which it is most difficult to estimate. The prudent course *is* to consider the end, count the cost, before adopting the course that desire suggests. But pleasures are so externally and accidentally connected with the performance of a deed, that attempt to foresee them is probably the stupidest course which could be taken in order to secure guidance for action. Suppose a man has a desire to visit a sick friend, and tries to determine the good by calculation of pleasures and pains. Suppose he is especially sensitive to the sight of suffering; suppose a disagreeable difference of opinion on some topic comes up in the course of the interview; suppose some bore turns up during the visit:—consider in short the multitude of accidental features of pleasure and pain which are wholly irrelevant to making a wise judgment as to what should be done. An indefinite number of extraneous circumstances affect the pleasures and pains which follow from an act, and have results which are quite foreign to the intrinsic and foreseeable consequences of the act.

We may, however, modify the line of reasoning somewhat, and confine the scope of the theory to pleasures and pains which so intrinsically accompany the nature of an act that they may be calculated. All of us get some pleasure by performing the acts which are congenial to our dispositions; such acts are, by conception, agreeable; they agree with, suit, our own tendencies. An expert in tennis likes to play tennis· an artist likes to paint pictures; a scientific man to investigate; a philosopher to speculate; a benevolent man to do kindly deeds; a brave man seeks out scenes in which endurance and loyalty may be exercised, etc. In such cases, given a certain structure of character and trend of aptitudes, there is an intrinsic basis for foreseeing pleasures and pains, and we may limit the theory to such consequences, excluding purely accidental ones.

But in modifying the theory in this way we have really set up the man's existing character as the criterion. A crafty, unscrupulous man, will get pleasure out of his sheer wiliness. When *he* thinks of an act which would bring pain in the experience of a generous frank person, he will find the thought a source of pleasure, and (so by the theory) a good act to perform. The same sort of thing will be true of the cruel, the dissolute, the malicious, person. The pleasures and pains each will foresee will be those which are in accord with his present character. Imagine two men who momentarily are taken by the idea of a harsh revenge upon a man who has inflicted ill treatment. For the moment both of them will get at least a passing pleasure from the image of the other man as overthrown and suffering. But the one who is kind-hearted will soon find himself pained at the thought of the harm the other man is experiencing; the cruel and revengeful person will glow with more and more pleasure the longer he dwells upon the distress of his enemy—if pleasure be a sign of goodness, the act will indeed be good to him.

There is thus a double misconception in the theory. Unconsciously, it slips in the criterion of the kind of pleasures which would be enjoyed by a man already good; the sort of pleasures which are taken to be normal. Other things being equal, pleasures are certainly a good to be enjoyed, not an evil to be shunned. But the phrase "other things being equal" covers a good deal of ground. One does not think of the pleasures of the dissolute, the dishonest, the mean and stingy, person, but of the pleasure of esthetic enjoyment, of friendship and good companionship, of knowledge, and so on. But there is no denying that characters we morally contemn get actual pleasure from *their* lines of conduct. We may think, and quite properly so, that they *ought* not to, but nevertheless they do. There are certain kinds of happiness which the good man enjoys which the evil-minded man does not—but the reverse is true. And this fact is fatal to the theory that pleasures constitute the good because of which a given object is entitled to be the end of action.

The other misconception consists in confusion of anticipated, prospective pleasure with the enjoyment immediately experienced in the thought of an end. Whenever a future object is thought of as an end, the thought arouses a *present* pleasure or discomfort. And any *present* enjoyment or disagreeableness strengthens or weakens the hold of its particular object upon our attention. It intensifies or reduces the *moving* force of the object thought of. A desire may be inflamed to a practically uncontrollable degree by dwelling upon the pleasures which the imagination of it *now* excites in me. But this increase of the dynamic motive power of the object has nothing to do with judgment, or foresight of the goodness of the consequences which *will* ensue if we take that object to be our end. Indeed, in many cases it is positively hostile to sound judgment of future consequences. The most which can be said is that after a man has judged that some end is good to attain, it is a wise act on his part to foster its pleasurable associations. In this way his resolution will be confirmed against distractions. A student who has decided to spend his evening in study will find his determination weakened if he continually permits his mind to dwell on the enjoyments he might have had by doing something else.

Hazlitt said that "pleasure is that which is so in itself. Good is that which approves itself on reflection, or the *idea* of which is a source of satisfaction. All pleasure is not therefore, morally speaking, equally a good; for all pleasure does not equally bear reflecting upon."

It is true that there is nothing good to us which does not include an element of enjoyment and nothing bad which does not contain an element of the disagreeable and repulsive. Otherwise the act or object is merely indifferent; it is passed by. But the statement that all good has enjoyment as an ingredient is not equivalent to the statement that all pleasure is a good. The quotation from Hazlitt points out the difference. If we judge, we often find that we cannot *approve* an enjoyment. This is not because the pleasure is itself evil but because judgment brings to light relations of the pleasure-giving act and object which we shrink from morally, or are ashamed of. An act appeals to us as pleasurable. If we stop to think we may find that the pleasure is due to something in ourselves which we feel to be unworthy, as to a mean or yellow streak. Or when we judge, we approve the enjoyment; not because it is in its isolation a good, but because upon examination we find that we are willing to stand by the conditions and the effects with which the pleasure is connected. Things give us pleasure because they are agreeable to (agree with or suit) something in our own make-up. When we reflect, we become aware of this connection: thus in the judgment to the moral value of an enjoyment we are really judging our own character and disposition. If you know what sort of things a man nds enjoyable and disagreeable you have a sure clew to his nature—and the principle applies to ourselves as well as to others.

The prudence or insight which constitutes, from the side of the goodness and badness of ends, the chief virtue is thus that which is exercised by an impartial and undisturbed spectator; by a man, not when he is undergoing the urge of a strong desire, but in a moment of calm reflection. In the latter case he judges the desire and its satisfaction as elements in a larger whole of conduct and character. There may well be as much difference in these two attitudes as there is between a man pushed by intense desire to the performance of a criminal act and the judge who passes upon his act. The important truth conveyed by the relation which exists between enjoyment and good is that we should integrate the office of the judge—of reflection—into the formation of our very desires and thus learn to take pleasure in the ends which reflection approves.

The conclusion we have arrived at is that there is important difference in the intrinsic quality of enjoyments, that a pleasure which does not "bear reflecting upon" is different in kind from one which does bear reflecting upon. While most hedonists have held that pleasures are alike, differing only in intensity and duration, John Stuart Mill introduced the idea of difference in quality. He said, "Human beings have faculties more elevated than animal appetites, and when once made conscious of them, do not regard anything as happiness that does not include their gratification."

"Few human creatures would consent to be changed into any of the lower animals, for a promise of the fullest allowance of a beast's pleasure; no intelligent human being would consent to be a fool, no instructed person would be an ignoramus, no person of feeling and conscience would be selfish and base, even though they should be persuaded that the fool, the dunce or the rascal is better satisfied with his lot than they are with theirs. . . . It is indisputable that the being whose capacities of enjoyment are low has the greatest chance of having them fully satisfied; and a highly endowed being will always feel that any happiness which he can look for, as the world is constituted, is imperfect. . . . It is better to be a human being dissatisfied than a pig satisfied; better to be a Socrates dissatisfied than a fool satisfied. And if the fool or the pig is of a different opinion, it is because he only knows his own side of the question. The other party to the comparison knows both sides."

Such a passage wins ready assent from moral common-sense. Yet its meaning is not wholly clear. There are persons who have "known" both higher and lower enjoyments who still choose the latter; they prefer, we may truly say, to be pigs. It is often easier to be a pig than to judge and act like a Socrates— and Socrates, one may remind oneself, came to death as a consequence of his "wisdom." In order that Mill's statement may be acceptable we must include *understanding* as part of the meaning of "knowing." In isolation, one enjoyment cannot be said to be higher or lower than another. There is nothing intrinsically higher in the enjoyment of a picture or an instructive book than there is in that of food—that is, when the satisfaction is taken apart from the bearings and relationships of the object in life as a connected whole. There are times when the satisfaction of hunger takes precedence of other satis- factions; it is at that time—for the time being—"higher." We conclude that the truth contained in Mill's statement is not that one "faculty" is inherently higher than another, but that a satisfaction which is seen, by reflection based on large experience, to unify in a harmonious way his whole system of desires is higher in quality than a good which is such only in relation to a particular want in isolation. The entire implica- tion of Mill's statement is that the satisfaction of the whole self in any end and object is a very different *sort* of thing from the satisfaction of a single and independent appetite. It is doing no violence to ordinary speech to say that the former kind of sat- isfaction is denoted by the term "happiness," and the latter kind by the term "pleasure," so that Mill's argument points not so much to a different quality in different pleasures, as it does to a difference in quality between an enduring satisfaction of the whole self and a transient satisfaction of some isolated element in the self.

We therefore not only may but must, in accordance with facts, make a distinction between pleasures and happiness, well- being, what Aristotle called *eudaimonia*. There is no such thing strictly speaking as *a* pleasure; pleasure is pleasant*ness*, an abstract noun designating objects that are pleasant, agreeable. And any state of affairs is pleasant or agreeable which is congenial to the existing state of a person whatever that may be.

What is agreeable at one time disagrees at another; what pleases in health is distasteful in fatigue or illness; what annoys or disgusts in a state of repletion is gratifying when one is hungry and eager. And on a higher scale, that which is pleasant to a man of generous disposition arouses aversion in a mean and stingy person. What is pleasant to a child may bore an adult; the objects that gratify a scholar are repulsive to a boor. Pleasantness and unpleasantness are accordingly signs and symptoms of the things which at a particular time are congenial to a particular make-up of the organism and character. And there is nothing in a symptom of the quality of an existing character which fits it to be a desirable end, however much it may serve as a guide or a warning.

There is something accidental in the merely agreeable and gratifying. They *happen* to us. A man may get pleasure by finding a sum of money on the street, eating a good dinner, running unexpectedly across an old friend. Or a man stumbles and falls, hurts himself and suffers pain; or, through no fault of his own he experiences an intensely disagreeable disappointment. It would be absurd to attribute goodness or badness in any moral sense to these things which have no intrinsic connection with deliberate action. There is nothing more productive of suffering than the loss of a dear friend, but no one thinks of the man who suffers the loss as thereby injured in character. A "lucky" man experiences pleasant objects to an unusual degree, but he may only be rendered obtuse, thoughtless and conceited because of that fact.

Happiness, on the contrary, is a stable condition, because it is dependent not upon what transiently happens to us but upon the standing disposition of the self. One may find happi-

ness in the midst of annoyances; be contented and cheerful
in spite of a succession of disagreeable experiences, if one has
braveness and equanimity of soul. Agreeableness depends
upon the way a particular event touches us; it tends to focus
attention on the self, so that a love of pleasures as such tends
to render one selfish or greedy. Happiness is a matter of the
disposition we actively bring with us to meet situations, the
qualities of mind and heart with which we greet and interpret
situations. Even so it is not directly an *end* of desire and effort,
in the sense of an end-in-view purposely sought for, but is
rather an end-product, a necessary accompaniment, of the
character which is interested in objects that are enduring and
intrinsically related to an outgoing and expansive nature. As
George Eliot remarked in her novel, *Romola*, "It is only a
poor sort of happiness that could ever come by caring very
much about our own narrow pleasures. We can only have the
highest happiness, such as goes along with being a great man,
by having wide thought and much feeling for the rest of the
world as well as ourselves; and this sort of happiness often
brings so much pain with it, that we can only tell it from pain
by its being what we would choose before everything else,
because our souls see it is good." [1]

Happiness as distinct from pleasure is a condition of the
self. There is a difference between a tranquil pleasure and
tranquillity of mind; there is contentment with external circumstances because they cater to our immediate enjoyment,
and there is contentment of character and spirit which is
maintained in adverse circumstances. A criterion can be
given for marking off mere transient gratification from true
happiness. The latter issues from objects which are enjoyable
in themselves but which also reënforce and enlarge the other
desires and tendencies which are sources of happiness; in

---

[1] That "happiness," so conceived, forms a *standard of judgment* rather than
an *end of desire* is a fact which is taken up in the Chapter on Approbation.
See pp. 101–104.

a pleasure there is no such harmonizing and expanding tendency. There are powers within us whose exercise creates and strengthens objects that are enduring and stable while it excludes objects which occasion those merely transient gratifications that produce restlessness and peevishness. Harmony and readiness to expand into union with other values is a mark of happiness. Isolation and liability to conflict and interference are marks of those states which are exhausted in being pleasurable.

§ 4. THE EPICUREAN THEORY OF GOOD AND WISDOM

We now pass on to another theory of the proper end of desire and thought—that known as the Epicurean. The versions we have been dealing with are occupied with *future* ends, the thought of which should regulate present desire and effort. But future enjoyments and sufferings are notoriously uncertain. They are contingent upon all sorts of external circumstances, of which even the most fundamental, the persistence of life itself, is highly precarious. Reflection upon the vicissitudes of life led therefore some observers to regard solicitude for the future as a source of worry and anxiety, rather than as a condition of attaining the good. There is no wisdom in finding good in what is exposed to circumstances beyond our control; such conduct is rather a manifestation of folly. The part of wisdom is then to cultivate the present moment as it passes, to extract from it all the enjoyment which it is capable of yielding. *Carpe diem.* The idea is poetically expressed in the lines of Edna St. Vincent Millay:

> "I burn my candle at both ends,
> It will not last the night;
> But ah, my foes, and oh, my friends
> It gives a lovely light—"

It is grossly expressed in the saying "Eat, drink and be merry, for tomorrow we die."

There is nevertheless on this theory great difference between a thoughtless grasping at the pleasures of the moment, and a reflectively regulated procedure. Experience teaches that some enjoyments are extremely fleeting and are also likely to be followed by reactions of discomfort and suffering. Such is the case with all extreme and violent pleasures. Indulgence in intense pleasure rarely pays; it is a liability rather than an asset. For experience shows that such a pleasure usually plunges us into situations that are attended with inconvenience and suffering. Those enjoyments which turn out to be *good* are calm and equable pleasures; experience discloses that these spring from intellectual and esthetic sources which, being within us, are within our control. Pleasures of the appetites, like sex, may be more intense, but they are not so enduring nor so likely to give rise to future occasions of enjoyment as those which come from books, friendship, the fostering of esthetic delight. Our senses and appetites are concerned with external things, and hence commit us to situations we cannot control. Of the delights of the senses, however, those of the eye and ear are better worth cultivating than those of taste and smell. For the former are more closely associated with intellectual pleasures, and also with conditions more common, more widely spread, in nature. Enjoyment of sunlight, moving waters, fresh air, is tranquil and easily obtainable. To entrust one's gratifications to objects of luxury is to commit one's self to troublesome search and probable disappointment. The simple life is the good life because it is the one most assured of present enjoyment. Private friendship is better than public life. For friends gather together naturally and foster harmony. To engage in public life is to put one's fortunes at the disposal of things beyond control, and to involve oneself in violent changes or at least continual vicissitudes.

This theory constitutes Epicureanism in its original form— a doctrine far removed from that surrender to voluptuous pleasures often associated with the name. Its maxim is to cherish those elements of enjoyment in the present which are most assured, and to avoid entanglement in external circumstances. This emphasis upon the conditions of security of *present* enjoyment is at once the strong and the weak point in the Epicurean doctrine.

The theory avoids the difficulties about foresight and calculation of future pleasures and pains which nullify the type of theory previously considered. It is a matter of experience, personal and social, that gentle and equable enjoyment is safer and more lasting than the vehement gratifications of excessive excitement. The person cultivated in books, intellectual pursuits, apt in friendly companionship, has sources of satisfaction more wholly within himself than has the person given to sensual pleasures or to the pursuit of money and fame. There is obviously sound sense in the maxim as far as it goes. The lesson is particularly needed in periods of bustle, hurry, and luxury, when men are carried away by interest in external and passing things, preoccupied with the material consequences of machinery and business and lose possession of themselves.

On the other hand, the doctrine is fundamentally one of withdrawal and restriction, even if it take the form of a high intellectual "disinterestedness," aloof from the ado and mêlée of practical affairs. If it were possible to isolate the present from the future, perhaps no better working rule for attaining happiness could be found. But the quality of selfish engrossment in one's own enjoyment which seems to cling to the doctrine is a necessary product of the attempt to exclude concern for the future. The doctrine is, ultimately, one of seclusion and passivity. It not only omits the enjoyment which comes from struggle against adverse conditions, with effort to achieve the difficult, but it is a doctrine of retreat from the scene of struggle in which the mass of men are perforce engaged. It is a doctrine which can appeal only to those who are already advantageously situated. It presupposes that there are others who are doing the hard, rough work of the world, so that the

[handwritten marginal note: Time moves from past to present]

[handwritten note at bottom: I don't see it implying those things at all!!! Nor is it exclusive and for the wealthy]

few can live a life of tranquil refinement. It is selfish because of what it excludes. It is a doctrine which will always flourish, though probably under some other name than Epicureanism, when social conditions are troubled and harsh, so that men of cultivation tend to withdraw into themselves and devote themselves to intellectual and esthetic refinement.

§ 5. SUCCESS AS THE END

A third variant of the theory that the chief moral demand is for wisdom in choice of ends is the doctrine of "success," understood in the sense of enlightened self-interest. This theory is not committed to any particular doctrine about pleasures and pains, and has rarely been formulated with the intellectual precision of the other principles. But it is widely acted upon in practice. It is hinted at in the saying that "honesty is the best policy." It tends to prevail in what are called practical affairs; business, politics, administration, wherever achievement and failure can be measured in terms of external power, repute, making money, and attainment of social status. The doctrine puts a high estimate on efficiency, on getting things done; it admires thrift, shrewdness, industriousness, and condemns laziness and stupidity. It is suspicious of art, save as an embellishment of practical success, and is distrustful of distinctively intellectual pursuits save when they bear tangible practical fruit.

In spite of the fact that moralists generally take a disparaging attitude toward this view of life, there is something to be said for it. Enlightened self-interest, planning and calculation for success, do not seem to rank very high as motives. But when one considers the amount of harm done by sheer ignorance, folly, carelessness, by surrender to momentary whim and impulse, one may safely conclude that the state of things would be better than it is if more persons were moved by intelligent interest in external achievement. And when we consider how much that has prided itself upon being moral has been content with mere "meaning well," with good intentions (which according to the saying help to "pave hell"), that are devoid of energy in action and efficiency in execution, one cannot withhold a modicum of respect for a doctrine that lays stress upon accomplishment, even if its standard of accomplishment is not high. Moreover there are comparatively few who can afford to despise reference to success in achievement. Students, engineers, professional men are likely to be steadied in their callings by regard for success. The maxim of prudence, interpreted to signify expediency in respect to achievement, at least tends to hold men to their work, and to protect them from distraction and waste of time and energy.

When all allowances are made, however, the defects of the doctrine are sufficiently obvious. It hardly rises above the more external aspects of life; it encourages the idea of "rising," of "getting on," of "making a go," while it accepts without question current estimates of what these things consist in. It does not criticize the scheme of values which happens to be current, say, in an age when men are devoted to pecuniary gain. It encourages conceiving of gain and loss in tangible material terms. The idea of success in the general sense of *achievement* is a necessary part of all morality that is not futile and confined to mere states of inner feeling. But the theory in question commits itself to a superficial, conventional, and unexamined conception of what constitutes achievement. It pins its faith to certain values at the expense of others more human and more significant. Morality must be "worldly" enough to take account of the fact that we live in a world where things have to be done. But that does not signify that achievement should be understood in a worldly-minded way.

§ 6. ASCETICISM AS THE END

Another interpretation of the nature of wisdom in the formation of ends and judgment of the good was put forth in Greece

by the Cynic school. As we have seen the great problem concerning ends is to discriminate between those which are "good"
in a near-by and partial view, and those which are enduringly
and inclusively good. The former are more obvious; the latter
depend upon the exercise of reflection and often can be discovered and sustained in thought only by reflection which is
patient and thorough. Even so, it is notorious that things
which are simply *judged* to be good are pallid and without
power to move us compared with warmer and nearer goods
which make a direct appeal to those impulses and desires that
are already urgent. Hence, the Cynic school thought it the
part of moral wisdom to treat practical exercises which form
stable habits as the important thing. Artisans and craftsmen
are skilful and persistent in pursuit of aims not in virtue of
reflection and theory, but because of habits formed by exercise. Why not carry the principle over into morals generally?
The great thing is to attain command over immediate appetite
and desire. Thinking is comparatively impotent in giving
this command; trained habit is potent. The moral maxim is
then to *practice* the right act till habit is firm.

In the precise form in which the theory was advanced by
the Cynic school it has not had great influence. But the underlying conception that wisdom consists in subjection and discipline of desire, and that this subordination is obtained by
deliberate exercise rather than by reflection, has become an important part of all those moral ideas which have a Puritanical
color. In the extreme form, the principle is called Asceticism
(from the Greek, ἄσκησις, exercise, discipline). Popularly,
the view is presumed to be opposed to the very idea of happiness and satisfaction. It does look with suspicion upon all
ordinary forms of gratification as morally dangerous. But it
does so in the interest of a final satisfaction of a different
type—as a martyr endures suffering in this world in the hope
of eternal happiness in another world, or if not that, then because of the satisfaction he obtains through being faithful to

his principles. Ordinary pleasures are deceptive; they mislead judgment and action. Their deceptive quality is what stands between us and the wisdom that lays hold of the true good. The pleasures of ordinary desire are so strong that the latter have to be subdued if we are to be loyal to real satisfaction. The way to subdue them is to engage systematically in exercises which are naturally uncongenial; then we harden ourselves to pain and steel ourselves against the seductions of desire. Repeated exercise moreover weakens the intensity of desire.

John Locke was no ascetic. Yet there is an ascetic element contained in his statement that "It seems plain to me that the principle of all virtue and excellency lies in a power of denying ourselves the satisfaction of our desires when reason does not authorize them." And he goes on to add, "This power is got by custom, made easy and familiar by an early practise. If therefore I might be heard I would urge that contrary to the ordinary way, children should be used to submit their desires and go without their longings even from their very cradles." [1] Nor was William James an ascetic. Yet in his discussion of Habit he says, "Keep the faculty of effort alive in yourself by a little gratuitous exercise every day. That is, be systematically ascetic or heroic in unnecessary points. Do every day or two something for no other reason than that you would rather not do it, so that when the hour of dire need draws nigh it may not find you unnerved and untrained to stand the test." [2]

It is impossible not to recognize an element of truth in such advice. Ends contemplated only in thought are weak in comparison with the urgencies of passion. Our reflective judgment of the good needs an ally outside of reflection. Habit is such an ally. And habits are not maintained save by exercise; they are not self-generated. They are produced only by

[1] *Of Education*, sec. 38.
[2] *Principles of Psychology*, I., p. 125.

a course of action which is persisted in, and the required persistence cannot be left to chance. It is not necessary to go to the extreme of ascetic doctrine and hold that there is something inherently beneficial in enduring pain and suppressing enjoyment. But it is a fact that some degree of unpleasantness is almost sure to attend the first performance of deeds that are done for the sake of forming a strong habit. "Discipline" is proverbially hard to undergo.

The criticism of this theory is in principle similar to that directed against both Epicureanism and the doctrine of successful policy. There is an element of truth in the idea that exercise is necessary to form habits strong enough to resist the solicitations of passion. But as in the case of cultivating immediate gentle pleasures and of aiming at achievement, this element of truth should be stated positively, not negatively. Instead of making the subjugation of desire an end in itself, it should be treated as a necessary function in the development of a desire which will bring about a more inclusive and enduring good. Few indeed at present go to the extremes of the early ascetics who looked with suspicion upon the family, state, art, and science since these may cater to sexual appetite, earthly ambition for power, or indulge the lust of the eye and the pride of intellect. But professed moralists still sometimes repel others, especially the young, from all morals by identifying morality with the negative for the sake of the negative, with restraint as itself an end.

There is not much danger in most circles in modern society that the ascetic principle will be taken seriously; there is, however, a real danger that it will affect the teaching of morals in some quarters to such a degree as to throw those taught over to the opposite extreme, and thus instigate them to take up with the doctrine that all inhibition is dangerous, and that every impulse should be "expressed" and every desire indulged. What is dangerous is not inhibition but those methods of trying to accomplish it which do not in fact

inhibit or control, but which merely cover the desire up from
consciousness, force it below observation and thought, and
thus encourage it to work in indirect and morbid channels.
All thought involves inhibition, if only that of delay until the
worth of a desire has been inquired into; usually it involves a
further control in which the original desire is subordinated
by being taken up into a larger purpose.

The error of the ascetic and the "free-expression" theories
is the same. It is the failure to see that the negative element
of restraint is valuable as a factor in the formation of a *new*
end and the construction of a new good. The important thing
is the realization of this new good, something to be attained by
positive means not by sheer endeavor to stamp out contrary
impulses. The larger good when dwelt upon alone has the
power to attenuate the force of opposed tendencies. The real
danger lies in dallying, in toying, with the immediately urgent
impulse, postponing decisive action in behalf of the approved
end. As James says, "No matter how full a reservoir of maxims one may possess . . . if one has not taken advantage of
every concrete opportunity to *act*, one's character may remain
entirely unaffected for the better. . . . Let the expression be
the least thing in the world—speaking genially to one's aunt,
or giving up one's seat in a horse car, if nothing more heroic
offers—but let it not fail to take place." What Milton calls
"fugitive and cloistered virtue" is fugitive because it is
cloistered, because it is not decisively acted upon when the
occasion presents itself. Genuine power is gained not by
exercises performed for their own sake, especially not by acts
of mere repression, but by exercise in the fields where power
is positively needed in order to accomplish results.

In its extreme and logical form the conception of ends which
dominates the theory under discussion has no great present
vogue. Discussion of it is still important, however, because
its underlying idea is perpetuated in the tendency to regard
morals as a set of special and separate dispositions. Moral

goodness is quite commonly divided off from interest in all
the objects which make life fuller, and is confined to a narrow
set of aims, which are prized too often merely because they involve inhibition and repression. Experience shows that the effect of this attitude is to keep attention fixed upon the things
which are thought to be evil. The mind becomes obsessed
with guilt and how to avoid it. In consequence, a sour and
morose disposition is fostered. An individual affected in this
way is given to condemnation of others and to looking for evil
in them. The generosity of mind which is rooted in faith in
human nature is stifled. Meanwhile, the positive interest in
ends which is the source of abundant power grows weak.
Normally, discipline comes about as a fruit of steady devotion
to ends that are of positive value. The person thoroughly
interested in an end—whether it be that of an art or a profession or calling—will endure hardship and repellant conditions because they are incidents of the pursuit of what is good.
He will find in the course of his pursuit sufficient opportunity
for exercise of the harder virtues. The man who can make a
sport out of his endeavor to break a bad habit will succeed,
while failure will await the person who concentrates his
effort upon the negative idea of mere abstinence. There is a
contrast between the natural goods—those which appeal to
immediate desire—and the moral good, that which is approved after reflection. But the difference is not absolute and
inherent. The moral good is some natural good which is sustained and developed though consideration of it in its relations;
the natural enjoyment which conflicts with the moral good is
that which accompanies some desire which persists because
it is allowed to sway action by itself, apart from the connections which reflection would bring to light.

§ 7. CONCLUSION: CULTIVATION OF INTERESTS AS THE END

We have seen that the idea of Ends and the Good is the
counterpart of the *intellectual* aspect of character and con-

duct. The difficulty in the way of attaining and maintaining practical wisdom is the urgency of immediate impulse and desire which swell and swell until they crowd out all thought of remote and comprehensive goods. The conflict is a real one and is at the heart of many of our serious moral struggles and lapses. In the main, solution is found in utilizing all possible occasions, when we are not in the presence of conflicting desires, to cultivate interest in those goods which we do approve in our calm moments of reflection. John Stuart Mill remarked that "the cultivated mind . . . finds sources of inexhaustible interest in all that surrounds it; in the objects of nature, the achievements of art, the imaginations of poetry, the incidents of history, the ways of mankind, past, present and their prospects in the future." There are many times when the cultivation of these interests meets with no strong obstacle. The habits which are built up and reënforced under such conditions are the best bulwarks against weakness and surrender in the moments when the reflective or "true" good conflicts with that set up by temporary and intense desire. The proper course of action is, then, to multiply occasions for the enjoyment of these ends, to prolong and deepen the experiences connected with them. Morality then becomes positive instead of a struggle carried against the seductive force of lesser goods. This course of action gives no guarantee against occurrence of situations of conflict and of possible failure to maintain the greater good. But *reflective* attachment to the ends which reason presents is enormously increased when these ends have themselves been, on earlier occasions, *natural* goods enjoyed in the normal course of life. Ideal ends, those sustained by thought, do not lose their ideal character when they are directly appreciated; in the degree in which they become objects of positive interest their power to control and move conduct in times of stress is reënforced.

This fact brings out the common element found in the criticism of the various points of view discussed in this chapter.

The truth hinted at in the hedonistic view of moral wisdom, (that it consists in foresight and calculation of future enjoyments and sufferings) is that *present* enjoyment may accompany the thought of remote objects when they are held before the mind. Its error lies in supposing that in reflection our ideas go out to future pleasures instead of to future objects. A man in order to cultivate good health does not think of the pleasures it will bring to him: in thinking of the various objects and acts which will follow from good health he experiences a *present* enjoyment, and this enjoyment strengthens his effort to attain it. As Plato and Aristotle said over two thousand years ago, the aim of moral education is to develop a character which finds pleasure in right objects and pain in wrong ends.

Something similar is to be said of wisdom or prudence viewed as a judgment of ends which are expedient or that mark "good policy." As far as the maxim emphasizes means and conditions that are necessary to achievement, thus taking morals out of the region of sentimental vaporing and fantasies, miscalled idealism, the principle is sound. Error lies in restriction of the domains of value in which achievement is desirable. It is folly rather than wisdom to include in the concept of success only tangible material goods and to exclude those of culture, art, science, sympathetic relations with others. Once a man has experienced certain kinds of good in a concrete and intimate way, he would rather fail in external achievement than forego striving for them. The zest of endeavor is itself an enjoyment to be fostered, and life is poor without it. As John Stuart Mill said "some things called expedient are not useful but in reality are one branch of the harmful." To due reflection, things sometimes regarded as "practical" are in truth highly impolitic and shortsighted. But the way to eliminate preference for narrow and shortsighted expediences is not to condemn the practical as low and mercenary in comparison with spiritual ideals, but to cultivate all possible opportunities for the actual enjoyment of the reflective values and to engage in the activity, the practice, which extends their scope.

The morally wise, accordingly, appreciate the necessity of doing, of "exercise." They realize the importance of habit as a protection against beguilement by the goods proposed by immediate desire and urgent passion. But they also apprehend that abstinence for the sake of abstinence, mortification of the flesh for the sake of mortification, is not a rational end. The important ally to doing is sense of power, and this sense of power is the accompaniment of progress in actual achievement of a positive good. Next, if not equal in importance (in some temperaments, superior), is the esthetic factor. A golfer or tennis player may enjoy his exercises because he appreciates the value of "form." Emerson speaks of the *elegance* of abstinence. Moderation is the associate of proportion, and there is no art without measure. The restraint that ensues from a sense of the fitness of proportion is very different in quality from that which is exercised for its own sake. To find excess disgusting is more efficacious than finding it wrong although attractive.

Finally, the underlying truth of what is called Epicureanism contains an element upon which we have insisted: the importance of nurturing the *present* enjoyment of things worth while, instead of sacrificing present value to an unknown and uncertain future. If this course is popularly thought of as mere self-indulgence, as selfish and destructive of consecutive striving for remote ends, it is because emphasis is laid upon the bare fact of enjoyment instead of upon the *values* enjoyed. Here as with the other principles discussed, the conclusion is the need of fostering at every opportunity direct enjoyment of the kind of goods reflection approves. To deny direct satisfaction any place in morals is simply to weaken the moving force of the goods approved by thought.

Our discussion has centered on the goods which approve themselves to the thoughtful, or morally "wise," person in their relation to the satisfactions which suggest themselves because of immediate and intense desire, impulse, and appetite. The office of reflection we have seen to be the formation of a judgment of value in which particular satisfactions are placed as integral parts of conduct as a consistent harmonious whole. If values did not get in one another's way, if, that is, the realization of one desire were not incompatible with that of another, there would be no need of reflection. We should grasp and enjoy each thing as it comes along. Wisdom, or as it is called on the ordinary plane, prudence, sound judgment, is the ability to foresee consequences in such a way that we form ends which grow into one another and reënforce one another. Moral folly is the surrender of the greater good for the lesser; it is snatching at one satisfaction in a way which prevents us from having others and which gets us subsequently into trouble and dissatisfaction.

Up to this point we have passed over the social conditions which affect the development of wise and prudent attitudes of mind. But it is clear that the education which one receives, not so much the formal schooling as the influence of the traditions and institutions of the community in which one lives, and the habits of one's associates, are a profound influence. The simplest illustration is that of a spoiled child. The person who is encouraged to yield to every desire as it arises, the one who receives constantly the help of others in getting what he wants when he wants it, will have to possess extraordinary intellectual powers if he develops a habit of reflective valuation. What is true on this personal scale is true on a wide social scale. The general social order may be such as to put a premium upon the kind of satisfaction which is coarse, gross, "materialistic," and upon attitudes which are in impatient haste to grab any seeming near-by good. This state of affairs is characteristic of many phases of American life today. Love of power over others, of display and luxury, of pecuniary wealth, is fostered by our economic régime. Goods that are more ideal, esthetic, intellectual values, those of friendship which is more than a superficial comradeship, are forced into subordination. The need of fostering the reflective and contemplative attitudes of character is therefore the greater. Above all, there is the need to remake social conditions so that they will almost automatically support fuller and more enduring values and will reduce those social habits which favor the free play of impulse unordered by thought, or which make men satisfied to fall into mere routine and convention. The great bulwark of wisdom in judging values is a just and noble social order. Said Santayana,

"Could a better system prevail in our lives a better order would establish itself in our thinking. It has not been for want of keen senses, or personal genius, or a constant order in the outer world, that mankind have fallen back repeatedly into barbarism and superstition. It has been for want of good character, good example, and good government. There is a pathetic capacity in men to live nobly if only they would give one another the chance. The ideal of political perfection, vague and remote as it yet is, is certainly approachable, for it is as definite and constant as human nature." [1]

In conclusion, we point out that the discussion enables us to give an empirically verifiable meaning to the conception of *ideal* values in contrast with *material* values. The distinction is one between goods which, when they present themselves to imagination, are approved by reflection after wide examination of their relations, and the goods which are such only because their wider connections are not looked into. We cannot draw up a catalogue and say that such and such goods are intrinsically and always ideal, and such and such other ones inherently base because material. There are circumstances under which enjoyment of a value called spiritual because it is associated with religion is mere indulgence; when its good, in other words, becomes one of mere sensuous emotion.

[1] *Reason in Science*, p. 320.

There are occasions when attention to the material environment constitutes the ideal good because that is the act which thoroughgoing inquiry would approve. In a general way, of course, we can safely point out that certain goods are ideal in character: those of art, science, culture, interchange of knowledge and ideas, etc. But that is because past experience has shown that they are the *kind* of values which are likely to be approved upon searching reflection. Hence a *presumption* exists in their favor, but in concrete cases only a presumption. To suppose that the higher ideal value inheres in them *per se* would result in fostering the life of a dilettante and mere esthete, and would relegate all goods experienced in the natural course of life to a non-moral or anti-moral plane. There is in fact a place and time—that is, there are relationships—in which the satisfactions of the normal appetites, usually called physical and sensuous, have an ideal quality. Were it not so, some form of asceticism would be the only moral course. The business of reflection in determining the true good cannot be done once for all, as, for instance, making out a table of values arranged in a hierarchical order of higher and lower. It needs to be done, and done over and over and over again, in terms of the conditions of concrete situations as they arise.   In short, the need for reflection and insight is perpetually recurring.

LITERATURE

Regarding the GOOD AND HAPPINESS, see Aristotle, *Ethics*, trans. by Peters, 1884, Book I. and Book X., chs. vi.-ix.; Paulsen, *System of Ethics*, 1899, pp. 268–286; Rickaby, *Aquinas Ethicus*, Vol. I., pp. 6–39; Rashdall, *The Theory of Good and Evil*, 1907; Eaton, *The Austrian Theory of Values*, 1930, ch. iv.; Perry, *The Moral Economy*, 1909, and *General Theory of Value*, 1926, especially chs. i.–iv., xx., xxi.; Hastings' *Dictionary of Ethics and Religion*, 1922, article on Summum Bonum by Shorey; Hobhouse, *The Rational Good*, 1921; Russell, *The Right to Be Happy*, 1927; Sturt, *Human Value*, 1923; Palmer, *The Nature of Goodness*, 1903; Sharp, *Ethics*, 1928, Book II. on the Good, and chs. xxii. and xxiii. on Self-sacrifice; references on Happiness in III. of Baldwin's *Dictionary of Philosophy and Psychology*, 1905.

Regarding HEDONISM, see for historical material, Watson, *Hedonistic Theories from Aristippus to Spencer*, 1895; Wallace, *Epicureanism;* Pater, *Marius the Epicurean;* Sidgwick, *History of Ethics*, chs. ii. and iv. For criticism and exposition of Hedonism, see Green, *Prolegomena to Ethics*, 1890, pp. 163–167, 226–240, 374–388; James, *Principles of Psychology*, 1890, II., pp. 549–559; Sidgwick, *Methods of Ethics*, 1901, pp. 34–47, Book II. and chs. xiii. and xiv. of Book III.; Bain, *Emotions and Will*, Part II., ch. viii.; Calkins, *The Good Man and the Good*, 1918, ch. v.; Everett, *Moral Values*, 1918, ch. iii.; Stapledon, *A Modern Theory of Ethics*, 1929, ch. iv.

An effective statement of the truth in EPICUREANISM is found in Fite, *Moral Philosophy*, 1925, ch. xiii. For ascetism, see Lecky, *History of European Morals*, 3rd ed., 1916. Lippmann, *A Preface to Morals*, 1929, ch. ix. For the ethics of success, see Plato, *Gorgias* and Book I. of the *Republic;* Sumner, *Folkways*, 1907, ch. xx.; Nietzsche, *The Will to Power.*

CHAPTER III

RIGHT, DUTY, AND LOYALTY

§ 1. THE IDEA OF THE RIGHT

THE theories discussed in the last chapter differ among themselves. But they agree in regarding Good as the central fact in morals and in believing the great problem of morals to be determination of those ends of desire and action which are truly or rationally good. There are, however, factors in morality which seem to be independent of any form of satisfaction. Children, for example, are constantly told to do right because it is right. Adults find themselves under obligations which are imperative and which nevertheless prevent the satisfaction of their desires. We find ourselves subject to authority, under law, bearers of responsibilities which we did not choose and which we must meet. There is a strain of authority and obligation in morality which is not, on its face at least, reducible to the conception of the good as satisfaction, even reasonable satisfaction, of desire. On a large scale, we are taught that the claims of law are superior to the solicitations of desire, and that it is an immoral principle, that of selfishness, which leads us to put happiness ahead of loyalty to these claims.

Since these factors are so prominent in conduct, there is, as we might expect, a type of theory which centers in them. Upholders of this type do not exclude reference to the Good, but they give Good a radically different meaning from the theories previously considered. They admit the existence of *a* good which consists in the satisfaction of desires, but they regard this as a non-moral good; in extreme forms of the theory as even an *anti*-moral satisfaction. The moral Good, according

64

to them, is that which is Right, that which accords with law and the commands of duty. Men *ought* to find satisfaction in heeding the dictates of the right. But such satisfaction is different in kind from that which springs from gratification of natural impulses and affections.

The conflict between the good and the right is acutely apparent in the cases in which social demands run counter to desire. A child wants to run on the grass; he is told that the lawn belongs to another and that he must not trespass. Flowers attract his notice and he wishes to pick them. He is told that they are the property of another, and that he must not steal. Such instances are of daily occurrence. The institutions and legal regulations of the community stand over against the wishes and satisfactions of an individual, imposing injunctions and bans upon him.

In everyday experience, this conflict between law and the duties it imposes occasions more conflicts than proceed from the disparity between the good of immediate craving and the good determined by reflection, such as was discussed in the last chapter. Obedience to parents and teachers is, for example, constantly demanded of the young. They find themselves under authority, personal, and that of rules. The principles of morality come home to them, not so much as the purposes and aims which wise foresight sets forth, as prohibitions and injunctions which claim authority in the name of right, law, and duty. The morally good to them is what is permissible, allowed, *licit;* the morally bad is that which is forbidden, illegitimate. The dominant aim and purpose which morals sets up is to obey rules, to respect authority, to be loyal to the right.

Now theorists who uphold the primacy of the concept of Ends, Good, and Insight, may reasonably object to this type of morals in its cruder forms; they may contend that it has no place in reflective morals, since it represents simply the power given by custom to some persons to direct the conduct of others. We shall assume without argument that the retort is valid against much of the use which is currently made of authority and obedience. But the underlying principle cannot be so readily disposed of. It is asserted by some that "right" signifies merely the road or path which leads to good.

Its authority is said to be borrowed from the good which the right course serves. Or it is asserted that the conflict is not between good and right, but between the lesser and the greater good, since laws represent a social good which is superior to private good, so that the problem is one of making persons see that the social good is their *own true* good. The first version, that the right is the way to the good, is in agreement with forms of speech which identify the right with the proper and suitable; we have to use means to attain ends, and some means are adapted to the end and others are not. The first are proper, fit, right; the second are wrong, improper, unsuitable. The other version of the primacy of Good emphasizes the fact that all human experience shows the inability of individuals to judge what is good without the experience of mankind embodied in laws and institutions. The experience of the individual is narrow; that of the race is wide. Laws in the main express the sober and considered judgment of the community as to what is really good for individuals; the authority of law is on this basis the authority of comprehensive and reflectively approved good.

Regarding the notion that the right is the means to the good, it may be said that it is certainly *desirable* that acts which are deemed right should in fact be contributory to good. But this consideration does not do away with the fact that the *concept of Rightness*, in many cases, is independent of the concept of satisfaction and good. When a parent says "this is right and therefore you should do it," it is to be hoped that the performance of the act will actually conduce to some good. But as an idea, "right" introduces an element which is quite outside that of the good. This element is that of *exaction*, *demand.* A direct road means the straight, the best, course; but it also signifies the regulated and ordered course. A person may admit, intellectually, that a certain act is foolish, in that it involves a sacrifice of a greater ultimate good to a lesser near-by one. But he may then ask: why not be foolish if I want to be? The idea of wrong introduces an independent factor: that the act is from the standpoint of moral authority a refusal to meet a legitimate demand. There has to be an idea of the authoritative claim of what is reasonable in order to convert the Good into the Right.

Much the same thing is to be said when it is urged that the seeming conflict is between the social good and the private good, or between a large and comprehensive good and a smaller good, where it is reasonable to choose the greater satisfaction instead of the lesser. The real difficulty is that the person involved in the conflict does not realize that the social good is a good, in any sense, for *him*. In order that he may do so, he must first recognize it as having an independent and authoritative claim upon his attention. The Good is that which attracts; the Right is that which asserts that we *ought* to be drawn by some object whether we are naturally attracted to it or not.

A type of theory, contrasting with that based upon desire and satisfaction, reverses, accordingly, the order of ideas characteristic of the latter. It often makes much, for example, of Reason and Rational Ideas. But the significance attached to the terms in the two theories differs radically. "Reason" is now thought of not as intelligent insight into complete and remote consequences of desire, but as a power which is opposed to desire and which imposes restrictions on its exercise through issuing commands. Moral judgment ceases to be an exercise of prudence and circumspection and becomes a faculty, usually termed conscience, which makes us aware of the Right and the claims of duty. Many theories of this type have not been content to proclaim that the concept of the Right is

independent of that of Good, but have asserted that the
Right as the Moral Good is something completely isolated
from all natural desires and satisfactions. They fall, accordingly, under the strictures already passed (p. 224) on conceptions which divide conduct into two isolated spheres, one
moral and one not, and which look with suspicion upon all
the natural affections and impulses. Our discussion will accordingly be directed to showing that it is possible to maintain the distinctness of the concept of right without separating
it from the ends and the values which spring from those desires
and affections that belong inherently to human nature.

§ 2. THE ORIGIN OF MORAL CLAIMS

Can we find a place for the moral authority of the demands
to which we are subject, a place which is distinct, on the one
hand, from mere coercion, from physical and mental pressure,
and which, on the other hand, does not set up a law of duty and
right that has nothing to do with the natural desires and
tendencies of our human constitution? Such is the problem
that confronts us. For, on the one hand, mere compulsion
has no moral standing. Persons may and do yield to the demands of arbitrary force simply because they will suffer if
they do not. But such yielding develops a slavish weakness
in them and an arrogant disregard of the rights of others in
those who have power. On the other hand, we split man into
two disconnected parts if we say that there is a law and principle of Duty which has nothing to do with our normal impulses and purposes and which yet is supreme over them.

The way out is found by recognizing that the exercise of
claims is as natural as anything else in a world in which persons are not isolated from one another but live in constant
association and interaction. A child may be subject to demands from a parent which express nothing but the arbitrary
wish of the latter, plus a power to make the child suffer if he
does not conform. But the claims and demands to which the

child is subject *need* not proceed from arbitrary will; they may issue from the very nature of family life in the relation which exists between parent and offspring. Then they do not come to the child as an external and despotic power, but as expressions of a whole to which he himself belongs. He is moved to respond by his affection for his parents, by his respect for their judgment; even when the demand runs contrary to his uppermost desire he still responds to it as to something not wholly alien. Because of inherent relationships persons sustain to one another, they are exposed to the expectations of others and to the demands in which these expectations are made manifest.

The case is perhaps even clearer if we consider the parent as one who is also subject to claims. These need not be voiced in explicit form by the child; they do not proceed consciously from him. But the parent who is conscientious feels that they are involved in the *parental relation*. Because of this human relationship, something is owed to the child even though (perhaps even more because) the latter is not able to formulate that claim in any express demand. So friends owe something to one another because of the very nature of the friendly relation. Citizens in a just state respond at their personal inconvenience to the demands of the state, not because the latter may bring physical pressure or mental coercion to bear upon them, but because they are members of organized society: members in such an intimate sense that the demands are not external impositions even when they run counter to the good which a present desire calls for. The claims of friendship are not always agreeable; sometimes they may be extremely irksome. But we should not hesitate to say that one who refused to meet them merely because they were troublesome was no true friend. If we generalize such instances, we reach the conclusion that Right, law, duty, arise from the relations which human beings intimately sustain to one another, and that their authoritative force springs from the very nature of the relation that binds people together.

This conclusion will be strengthened if we consider in some detail the theories which explain moral authority and rightfulness on other grounds. Some of these conceptions make the will of God the *locus* of authority; others (like that of Thomas Hobbes) transfer it from God to the political State; Kant, in reaction against any external source, found it in a law of practical reason resident in man but having an entirely different origin and constitution from his impulses and affections. A popular version of the same underlying idea is that man has a double nature, being both spiritual and carnal, and that the flesh is rightfully subject to the law of the spirit. From the standpoint of history, it is worth noting that while the Greeks developed the idea of the Good and of moral insight, it was the Romans, with their strong legal and administrative talents, who made central the idea of authorization by law. The three maxims in which Roman moralists and jurists summed up the moral code all take the form of duties. Render to every other man that which is his due. So use what is your own as not to injure others. *Vivere honestum:* that is, live so as to deserve good repute from others. These maxims were said to be the essentials of the "law of nature," from accord with which the rightfulness of human insti utions and laws is derived.

§ 3. THE KANTIAN THEORY

Undoubtedly the most logically extreme formulation of the belief that authority and law come first, and that the conception of the good, in a moral sense, is secondary, is that of Kant. The subordination of Good to the Right is summed up in the words "the concept of good and evil must not be determined before the moral law, but only after it and by means of it." Nor does Kant stop here. He carries to its logical extreme that notion of the opposition between all the values which satisfy desires and the true moral good referred to in the previous chapter (p. 32). He accepts the hedonistic psychology with respect to desires. From the standpoint of desire, all good is a pleasure which is personal and private. The man who allows desires, even those of affection for others, to direct his conduct is, in final account, only seeking his *own* good, that is, his own pleasure. The ruling principle of all desires is Self-love, a development of the instinct for self-preservation which according to him governs all appetite and impulse. Thus the moral good is not only different from the natural goods which man experiences in the regular course of living but is *opposed* to them. The essence of the moral struggle is to put regard for moral law in the place of desire for satisfaction as the dominant maxim and motive of conduct. Morality is a struggle just because men in their native make-up and capacity naturally seek to satisfy their desires, while their higher nature imposes a complete check on this tendency.

Kant expressed the idea of the supreme authority of the concepts of law and duty so logically that his views are worthy of particular attention by means of a few examples. Natural impulse suggests to a mother care of her infant; but to be *morally good*, the motive of her conduct must be reverence for the moral law which makes it her bounden duty to care for the child. The view has been caricatured by saying that to be truly moral, the mother must suppress her natural affection. This extreme result is not implied. But it is no caricature to say that, according to Kant, the parent must suppress the tendency of natural affection to become the *motive* for performance of acts of attention to offspring. She must bring, as far as the moving spring of her actions is concerned, her affection *under* a deliberate appreciation of the *obligatory* nature of what she does. Her act is not morally good because it flows from affection, nor because it promotes the welfare of the young as its consequence. Again, a man engaged in service of a client is moved either by ambition for professional success or by acquired professional habits to do the best he can for the affairs of clients entrusted to his charge. But his acts are morally good—are *right* as distinct from satisfactory—only when such motives as affect his conduct, including even the wish to be of service to others, are subordinated to reverence for the moral law. Again, a merchant may supply customers with proper commodities, give honest change, serve them zealously, just because he thinks it good policy. He is only looking out for number one, while he *ought* to be doing what he does because it is a moral duty to act in that way.

One aspect of Kant's theory has been incidentally touched upon before (p. 16); namely, the contrast which is set up between will, defined as motive, and consequences; together with the attribution of moral goodness to the former alone. We shall here confine ourselves accordingly to that one element which is peculiar to his position; namely, the conception of reverence for law and duty as the only *justifying* motive. The law according to Kant is imperative; and the imperative command is absolute, unconditioned—the "categorical imperative," he calls it, in order to distinguish it from requirements of prudence and skill which are only hypothetical. The latter take the form: *If* you wish good health, or success in your calling, you *must* do so and so. The moral command says, You *must* act from the motive of duty, anyway. The extreme and logical form in which Kant states the principle of Right as distinct from the Good, of Law and Duty, brings out the difficulty in all theories which separate the right entirely from satisfaction of desires and affections. Ignoring technicalities in the Kantian theory, the difficulty is this: When all regard for consequences and for all ends which desire sets before us is excluded, what concrete material is left to be included within the idea of duty? Why may not a man go ahead in any line of conduct provided he is persuaded that his duty lies there? What saves him from self-deceit, from fanaticism, from cruel disregard of the interest of others, once he decides, apart from consideration of consequences, that something is his duty and is commanded by the moral law? Putting the question in its precise form, how shall a man go from the idea of duty in general to that of some particular act or mode of conduct as dutiful?

Kant recognizes the difficulty, and fancies he has an adequate answer to it. He does not blink the fact that the idea of Duty in general is without any particular content of its own. We are not aware, according to him, that any particular act is obligatory; we are only aware that it is our imperative duty to make the law of duty supreme in conduct. In itself this law of Duty is, he claims rather than merely admits, formal and empty. For all particular ends have to do with consequences and are linked up with desires. Where then is there any road from Duty in general to the knowledge that it is our duty to pursue some actual concrete end?

His answer takes the following form: The consciousness of duty is imposed upon us by our moral reason. We are not mere creatures of appetite and desire, of sense and nature, but there is within us a rational faculty which rises above desire and nature. It is the essence of Reason to express itself in universal and necessary terms. This trait implies that it is wholly self-consistent or universal. It does not say one thing at one time and another at another time; it does not vary with circumstances. So all that is required to know our duty in a particular case is to ask ourselves if the motive of that act can be made universal without falling into self-contradiction. For example:

"May I, when in distress, make a promise with the intention not to keep it? . . . The shortest way, and an unerring one to discover the answer to the question whether a lying promise is consistent with duty, is to ask myself, Should I be content that my maxim (to extricate myself from trouble by a false promise) should hold good as a universal law, for myself as well as for others? And should I be able to say to myself, every one may make a deceitful promise when he finds himself in a difficulty from which he cannot otherwise extricate himself? Then I personally become aware that while I can will the lie, I can by no means will that lying should be a universal law. For with such a law there would be no such thing as a promise. No one should have any faith in the proffered intention, or, if they do so over hastily, would pay one back in one's own coin at the first opportunity."

The principle if made universal simply contradicts itself, and thus reveals that it is no principle at all, not rational. Summing this up in a formula, we get as our standard of right action the principle: "Act as if the maxim of thy action were to become by thy will a universal law of nature."

It is not easy to do justice to Kant's formula without going into a consideration of the place which "Reason" occupies in his whole system. But it can be pointed out that in passing from the general and formal command of Reason over to judgment on the rightfulness or dutifulness of the particular case, there is an unconscious and yet complete shift in the conception of the work of reason. It is perfectly true that if a person considers the purpose or motive of his act in isolation, as if it were not a member of *Conduct* as a linked series of actions (p. 11), there is no rationality or reasonableness in his act. There is no principle or law because there is nothing which binds different acts together. Each act is a complete law unto itself, which is the same as no law at all. It *is* the part of reason to lead us to judge: Would I be willing to act for this end always and under all circumstances? Would I be willing to have others treat me according to it under similar circumstances? In Kant's language: Am I willing to have it made "universal," or am I seeking some special exception for myself under particular circumstances?

But this method instead of excluding all reference to consequences is but a way of securing impartial and general consideration *of* consequences. It does not say: Ignore consequences and do your duty because moral law, through the voice of reason, commands it. It says: Consider as widely as possible the consequences of acting in this way; imagine the results if you and others always acted upon such a purpose as you are tempted to make your end, and see whether you would then be willing to stand by it. If you proceed in this manner, you will get light upon the real character of your particular purpose at the moment. You will be aided in finding where your duty lies. And if a man discovers upon reflection that he would not like to be "paid back in his own coin," in as far as he is fair-minded (and in popular usage, fair-mindedness and rationality of judgment are synonymous terms) he will perceive the wrongness of his proposed act.

That in reality, although not in formal theory, Kant's universality signifies regard for social consequences instead of disregard of all consequences appears in another formula of the moral law which he sets forth. According to his view, the moral or rational will is an end in itself, not a means to something else. Now *every* person is equally an end in himself. Indeed, this is the very quality which marks off a person from a mere thing. Things we use as means; we subordinate physical objects and energies to our own special purposes; stones, timber, heat, electricity. But when we make another person a means to our ends, we violate his very being; we treat him as a slave and reduce him to the status of a merely physical object, or of a domestic animal, a horse or cow. Hence the moral law may be stated in the following form: "So act as to treat humanity, whether in thine own person or in that of any other, as an end, never as a means only." The person who makes a lying promise to another uses that other person as a means to his own profit. The man who proposes suicide treats personality in himself as merely a means to avoiding discomfort and trouble. This second formula is equivalent to a third and final principle: Since all human beings are equally persons and of equal claim upon the conduct of all, the ideal of rational conduct in observance of duty leads to the idea of a kingdom of ends. The moral law demands "the union of different rational beings in a system by common laws."

If we bear this outcome in mind, and think of the claims of others to whom we are bound in social relations, we are enabled to see in what respect the idea of Right and Duty is distinct from that of the Good, and yet how the two are connected.

In case of conflict of personal good with the good of others, most persons have a strong tendency to estimate their own satisfaction as having the higher value. There is no doubt that serious moral problems arise when that which we judge to be good because it is agreeable to our own desires comes into conflict with that which, if our own interests were not deeply involved, we should see to be the good of others. To regard oneself as one among others and not as the "only pebble on the beach," and to carry out this estimate in practice is perhaps the most difficult lesson we have to learn. If others did not put forth their claims and if these general claims were not embodied in a system of general social expectations, demands, and laws, he would be an exceptional individual indeed who should give only the same weight to his own good, as dictated by his own wants and purposes, as he gives to that of others. The urgency, intimate and close-by character of our own good operate strongly against our giving due heed to the welfare of others; in comparison, this seems to him pale, remote, negligible.

But the supposition of complete isolation is contrary to fact. Others do not leave us alone. They actively express their estimates of good in demands made upon each one of us. They accompany them with virtual promise of aid and support if their expectations are met, and with virtual threats of withdrawal of help, and of positive infliction of penalty, if we do not then take them into account in forming the purposes which control our own conduct. And these demands of others are not just so many special demands of so many different individuals. They are generalized into laws; they are formulated as standing claims of "society" in distinction from those of individuals in their isolated severalty. When considered as claims and expectations, they constitute the Right in distinction from the Good. But their ultimate function and effect is to lead the individual to broaden his conception of the Good; they operate to induce the individual to feel that nothing is good for himself which is not also a good for others. They are stimuli to a widening of the area of consequences to be taken into account in forming ends and deciding what is Good.

This conclusion confers an independent standing upon the conception of Right, and yet makes clear its ultimate moral connection with the conception of the Good. It preserves Right from being arbitrary and formal and Good from being narrow and private. But the whole problem is not yet disposed of. Reflective morality asks: What about the rightfulness of specific claims and demands that are put forth by society, especially by those in authority? Are they, in the concrete forms in which they are put forth, claims and expectations which *should* be exercised? What is the connection, for example, between a particular injunction or prohibition of parent or governmental official and the general notion of right which it claims to embody? What is *its* moral justification?

§ 4. THE JUSTIFICATION OF A CLAIM

The question is not a purely speculative one. Children in the family, citizens and groups in the State, may feel that the demands to which they are socially subject are arbitrary and lacking in genuine moral authority. They may feel that current laws spring from past customs which are outworn, or that they represent the *force* of those in power rather than a moral ideal. A parent's, teacher's, ruler's injunction "Do this" may turn out on reflection to be the expression of *his* impulse, or a manifestation of his personal interest in his *own* power and privilege, a manifestation backed up by his superior position rather than by ethical principle. Obedience is often procured by the use of rewards and penalties, promises and threats: by what in moral theory have come to be called "sanctions." And if the ultimate "reason" for observance of law and respect for duty lies in the hope of reward and fear of penalty, then the "right" is nothing but a round-about means to the hedonistic end of private satisfaction. Morality becomes servile; a condition of apparent obedience may signify in fact nothing but a state of fear. Moreover, the situation leads to a kind of clever hypocrisy. An individual may be clever enough to get his own way, while so covering up his tracks that he seems loyal to constituted authority.

The same point comes out when the situation is viewed in reverse. A shrewd observer of political life remarked that power is poison. It is difficult for a person in a place of authoritative power to avoid supposing that what he wants is right as long as he has power to enforce his demand. And even with the best will in the world, he is likely to be isolated from the real needs of others, and the perils of ignorance are added to those of selfishness. History reveals the tendency to confusion of private privilege with official status. The history of the struggle for political liberty is largely a record of attempt to get free from oppressions which were exercised in the name of law and authority, but which in effect identified loyalty with enslavement. With the concentration of alleged moral authority in the few, there is a corresponding weakening of judgment and the power to accept responsibility on the part of the many. "Morality" gets reduced to carrying out orders.

The discussion brings to light an underlying problem. What is the ultimate nature of moral authority? What differentiates it from habitual custom or from command of power? The problem as we have seen is not merely theoretical; it has its practical side. Men of affairs, those in position of power, executives and administrators, are constantly under the temptation to view laws as ends in themselves, and to think that the Right is made secure through the issuing of rules and regulations and by securing conformity to them. Even when the ruler is the mass of the people, as in a democracy, the danger remains. Is there not a saying, "*Vox populi, vox dei?*" That law exists for man and not man for law is not an easy lesson to learn, nor is the difficulty lessened when in reaction against authority which seems repressive and arbitrary, there is recourse to the anarchy of individual appetite and impulse.

In short, while Right as an idea is an independent moral conception or "category," this fact does not solve the question of *what* is right in particular. Law and lawfulness are not all one with *a* law. Law is necessary because men are born and live in social relationships; *a* law is always questionable, for it is but a special means of realizing the function of law in general, namely, the institution of those relations among men which conduce to the welfare and freedom of all.

Individuals are interdependent. No one is born except in dependence on others. Without aid and nurture from others, he would miserably perish. The material of his intellectual subsistence, as well as of his physical, comes to him from others. As he matures, he becomes more physically and economically independent; but he can carry on his calling only through coöperation and competition with others; he has needs which are satisfied only through exchange of services and commodities. His recreations as well as his achievements are dependent upon sharing with others. The idea that individuals are born separate and isolated and are brought into society only through some artificial device is a pure myth. Social ties and connections are as natural and inevitable as are physical. Even when a person is alone he thinks with language that is derived from association with others, and thinks about questions and issues that have been born in intercourse. Independence of character and judgment is to be prized. But it is an independence which does not signify separateness; it is something displayed in relation to others. There is no one, for example, of whom independent inquiry, reflection, and insight are more characteristic than the genuine scientific and philosophic thinker. But his independence is a futile eccentricity unless he thinks upon problems which have originated in a long tradition, and unless he intends to share his conclusions with others, so as to win their assent or elicit their corrections. Such facts are familiar and commonplace. Their meaning is not always so definitely recognized:— namely, that the human being is an individual because of and in relations with others. Otherwise, he is an individual only as a stick of wood is, namely, as spatially and numerically separate.

Many of these relations are enduring, or recur frequently. The relation of child and parent, for example, lasts for a number of years, giving rise to claims for protection and nurture, and for attention, respect, and affection. The duties which express these relations are intrinsic to the situation, not enforced from without. The one who becomes a parent assumes by that very fact certain responsibilities. Even if he feels these to be a burden and seeks to escape from them, he flees from something which is part of himself and not from something imposed by external force. Many of the duties recognized in our system of common law arose out of relations which recur pretty constantly in the economic relations of men, as, for example, those of landlord and tenant, vendor and purchaser, master and servant, trustee and beneficiary. It does not follow from this fact that the duties expressing the relation have always been just what they should be; the relation may have been one-sided rather than reciprocal.

But the remedy lies not in the abolition of all duties but in a change in the character of the relationship.

While particular rights and duties may, then, be arbitrary there is nothing arbitrary or forced in the existence of right and obligation. The Romans spoke of duties as *offices*. An office is a function which has a representative value; that is, it stands for something beyond itself. It is as a parent, not just as an isolated individual, that a man or woman imposes obligations on children; these grow out of the office or function the parent sustains, not out of mere personal will. When they express merely one will in opposition to another, instead of proceeding from the tie which binds persons together, they violate their own basis. In the case of those persons who are usually called officers the point is even clearer. The legislator, judge, assessor, sheriff, does not exercise authority as his private possession, but as the representative of relations in which many share. He is an organ of a community of interests and purposes. In principle, therefore, Right expresses the way in which the good of a number of persons, held together by intrinsic ties, becomes efficacious in the regulation of the members of a community.

The fact that the idea or principle of Right has such a natural basis and inevitable rôle does not, however, signify that it will not conflict with what an individual judges to be his good and his end, nor does it guarantee the rightfulness of all claims and demands that are put forth in its name. On the contrary, one may use the power and prestige which a representative capacity confers to advance one's personal interests, add to one's individual enjoyments, and enhance one's private gains. A parent may degrade the parental office into a means of increasing his own comfort and displaying his own whims, satisfying his love of power over others. And so with civic and political officials. Such conduct is *faithlessness*, but such betrayal is unfortunately a common event. The evil extends; it provokes resentment against all authority, and the feeling grows that all duties are limitations of personal freedom and arbitrary impositions of superior power.

The conflict affects the interpretation of the meaning of law. On one hand, it is regarded as the expression of a superior will in reference to the wills of those whose wills are inferior and subject. On the other hand, it is erected into an impersonal and independent entity, above all human wills. Kant virtually defined the moral law in this fashion, although he did so in the professed name of a rational will. Undoubtedly the tendency to treat law as something in itself, over and above of all human relations instead of as an expression of the end and good which these relations should serve, has arisen in part at least because of a feeling that human relations fluctuate, and from the desire to find something stable and constant. This motive is implicit when the "majesty" and "sublimity" of law are spoken of. But the logical consequence and the practical effect, if the belief is acted upon, is to render morals harsh, because of neglect of the relation between law and obligation and the attainment of Good. It subjects the mass of men to the desires of those who have it in their power to declare and enforce what they take to be law.

The outcome of the discussion is that while Right in general has an independent status because of the social claims which attend human relations, any *particular* claim is open to examination and criticism. Is it entitled to claim the authority of right for itself? Is it truly rightful? To answer such questions and to guide judgment in criticism a criterion for the rightfulness of particular laws and obligations has to be found. The essence of the claim which Right puts forth is that even if the thing exacted does not appeal as his good to the one to whom it is addressed, he *should* voluntarily take it to be a good; that, in short, it should *become* his good, even if he does not so judge it at the time. This element of the "should" or "ought" is what differentiates the idea of Right from that of Good. But it does not cut the idea wholly loose from that of Good, for what "should be" is that an individual should *find* the required conduct good. The solution of the apparent contradiction between that which is not now judged good and yet *should* be judged good points the way to the criterion of which we are in search. Does the conduct alleged to be obligatory, alleged to have the authority of moral law behind it, actually contribute to a good in which the one from whom an act is demanded will *share?* The person upon whom the duty is laid himself makes claims upon others; he expects benefits from others; he holds others to the duties which they owe him, because of his ends and the values which he seeks to obtain. If the claim is, then, of the kind which he himself puts forth, if it serves a good which he prizes for himself, he must, in the degree in which he is fair-minded, acknowledge it to be a common good, and hence binding upon his judgment and action.

The point comes out perhaps most clearly if we ask what it is which makes an act wrong. Our theory commits us to the conclusion that a choice and deed are not wrong *merely* because they fail to conform with current laws and the customary code of duties. For these may be wrong, and an individual may have Right on his side in refusal to conform. Some persons persecuted as moral rebels in one period have been hailed as moral heroes at a later time; children build monuments to those whom their fathers stoned. Yet this fact does not commit us to the conclusion that there is no criterion of right and wrong except that personal subjective opinion sometimes improperly called private conscience. A man would not steal if there were no value placed by him on property; even a thief resents having what he has stolen taken from him. If there were no such thing as good faith, there could be no fraud. The wrongdoer counts upon good faith and honesty in others; otherwise there would be nothing beneficial to him in violating these ties. Wrong consists in faithlessness to that upon which the wrongdoer counts when he is judging and seeking for what is good to him. He betrays the principles upon which he depends; he turns to his personal advantage the very values which he refuses to acknowledge in his own conduct towards others. He contradicts, not as Kant would have it, some abstract law of reason, but the principle of reciprocity when he refuses to extend to others the goods which he seeks for himself. The justification of the moral non-conformist is that when he denies the rightfulness of a particular claim he is doing so not for the sake of private advantage, but for the sake of an object which will serve more amply and consistently the welfare of all. The burden of proof is upon him. In asserting the rightfulness of his own judgment of what is obligatory, he is implicitly putting forth a social claim, something therefore to be tested and confirmed by further trial by others. He therefore recognizes that when he protests he is liable to suffer the consequences that result from his protesting; he will strive with patience and cheerfulness to convince others.

If patience, cheerfulness, freedom from conceit, self-display, and self-pity are demanded of the moral non-conformist, there is a correlative duty imposed upon conformists: namely, the duty of toleration. History shows how much of moral progress has been due to those who in their own time were regarded as rebels and treated as criminals. The heart of reflective morality *is* reflection, and reflection is sure to result in criticism of some matters generally accepted and in proposals for variation of what is currently regarded as right. Toleration is thus not just an attitude of good-humored indifference. It is positive willingness to permit reflection and inquiry to go on in the faith that the truly right will be rendered more secure through questioning and discussion, while things which have endured merely from custom will be amended or done away with. Toleration of difference in moral judgment is a duty which those most insistent upon duty find it hardest to learn

As soon as one enemy of inquiry and public discussion is over-come, new enemies with new plausible reasons for exercising censorship and suppression of thought arise. And yet without freedom of thought and expression of ideas, moral progress can occur only accidentally and by stealth. Mankind still prefers upon the whole to rely upon force, not now exercised directly and physically as it was once, but upon covert and indirect force, rather than upon intelligence to discover and cling to what is right.

§ 5. THE SENSE OF DUTY

Corresponding to the generalized form in which demands are made there grows up a generalized sense of Duty—a sense of being bound by that which is right because of its rightful-ness. At first, duties are connected with specific relations, like those of a child to his parents, to his brothers and sisters. But with increasing moral maturity, there develops a sense of obligation in distinction from any particular situation. While a general idea arises out of the recurrence of special situations, it is more than a mere extract from them. It constitutes also a new attitude toward further special situa-tions. A person may use a variety of things in succession as if they were tables. When he has the general idea of a table, he is in possession of a *principle* of action. He can use his idea as an ideal, as something by which to criticize existing tables, and by which, under changed conditions, to invent a new table. One might warm himself by a fire a thousand times without having it occur to him to *make* a fire when he is cold. When he has the general idea of a fire, he has something which is emancipated from any given case and which may be employed to generate a fire when there is none in actual existence. So a person with a general conception of duty will have a new attitude; he will be on the lookout for situa-tions in which the idea applies. He will have an ideal or standard to which he must bring up particular cases.

While general ideas are of utmost value in the direction and enlargement of conduct, they are also dangerous: they tend to be set up as fixed things in themselves, apart from reference to any particular case. Such is the case when there develops the idea of "duty for the sake of duty." Here the notion of duty is isolated from the demands of special situations and is made a fetish. Conformity to the letter of the law then takes the place of faithfulness to its spirit—to its usefulness in calling attention to the good which is wider than that of immediate convenience or strong appetite. Duty is made to take precedence of all human claims, instead of operating as a reminder to consider human claims in a large way. The proper function of a general sense of duty is to make us sensitive to the relations and claims involved in particular situations, and this sensitiveness is especially needed whenever some immediate solicitation of desire tends to blind us to everything but itself. A generalized sense of right is a support in times of temptation; it gives a reënforcing impetus in carrying us over a hard place in conduct. A mother is habitually attentive to the claims of her offspring. Nevertheless, cases arise when it is much easier for her to put her own comfort first. A generalized sense of right and obligation is a great protection; it makes the general habit consciously available. But such a general sense as this grows out of occasions when the mother was faithful because she was actuated by direct affection for the child and direct interest in his welfare. A sense of duty is a weak staff when it is not the outcome of a habit formed in whole-hearted recognition of the value of the ties involved in concrete cases.

A sense of a common value and interest binding persons together is therefore the normal support and guide. But we are all of us subject to conditions in which we tend to be insensitive to this value, and where the sense of what is due others is weak in comparison with the force of a contrary inclination. The claims of others then find a valuable ally in a generalized sense of right and obligation which has been growing up because of previous appreciations of concrete relations.

In the final part of our discussion of the Good and moral wisdom, we noted that different social environments operate very differently in building up the power of good practical judgment. The same thing is true, and perhaps in even a greater degree, of the relation of social institutions to fostering loyalty, faithfulness, to the Right. There are social institutions which promote rebellion or at least indifference. Some tend to produce a specious, a conventional, or even hypocritical, loyalty. This happens when fear of suffering if one does not conform, is the leading consideration. Some social conditions foster external acknowledgment of duty at the expense of personal and critical judgment of ends and values. Other conditions induce men to think about what is truly right, and to create new forms of obligation. At present, without doubt, the social scene is so complex and so subject to rapid change, that its effect is distracting. It is hard to find any compass which will give steady guidance to conduct. In consequence the demand for a truly reflective, a thoughtful, morality was never so great. This is almost the only alternative to either moral drifting or else to unreasoning and dogmatic insistence upon arbitrary, formal codes held up as obligatory for no reason except that custom and tradition have laid complete hold upon us.

There is perhaps always a tendency to overestimate the amount of strict adherence to moral standards in the past and to exaggerate the extent of contemporary laxity. Nevertheless, changes in domestic, economic, and political relations have brought about a serious loosening of the social ties which hold people together in definite and readily recognizable relations. The machine, for example, has come between the worker and the employer; distant markets intervene between producer and consumer; mobility and migration have invaded and often broken up local community bonds; industries once carried on in the home and serving as a focus for union in the household have gone to the factory with its impersonal methods, and the mother as well as the father has followed them; the share of the family in the education of the young has become less; the motor car, the telephone, and new modes of amusement have placed the center of gravity in social matters in contacts that are shifting and superficial.   In countless ways the customary loyalties that once held men together and made them aware of their reciprocal obligations have been sapped.   Since the change is due to alteration of conditions, the new forms of lawlessness and the light and loose way in which duties are held cannot be met by direct and general appeal to a sense of duty or to the restraint of an inner law.   The problem is to develop new stable relationships in society out of which duties and loyalties will naturally grow.

LITERATURE

Kantian theory of Duty, *Theory of Ethics*, trans. by Abbott; *cf.* in Bradley, *Ethical Studies*, 1904, 1927, chapter on Duty for Duty's Sake; Clutton-Brock, *The Ultimate Belief*, and Otto, *Things and Ideals*, 1924, ch. iii.; Green, *Prolegomena to Ethics*, 1890, pp. 315–320, 381–388.   For opposite view, Guyau, *Sketch of Morals, without Obligation or Sanctions.*

For utilitarian interpretation of duty, see Bentham, *Principles of Morals and Legislation;* Bain, *Emotions and Will;* Spencer, *Principles of Ethics*, especially Vol. I., Part I., ch. vii.

GENERAL DISCUSSION: McGilvary, *Philosophical Review*, Vol. XI., pp. 333–352; Sharp, *Ethics*, 1928, Book I. on the Right, and *International Journal of Ethics*, Vol. II., pp. 500–513; Adler, *An Ethical Philosophy of Life*, 1918; Calkins, *The Good Man and the Good*, 1918, ch. i.; Driesch, *Ethical Principles in Theory and Practice*, trans. 1930, pp. 70–190; Everett, *Moral Values*, 1918, ch. ix. or Duty and ch. xi. on law.

CHAPTER IV

APPROBATION, THE STANDARD AND VIRTUE

§ 1. APPROVAL AND DISAPPROVAL AS ORIGINAL FACTS

CONDUCT is complex. It is so complex that attempts to reduce it intellectually to a single principle have failed. We have already noted two leading considerations which cut across each other: ends which are judged to satisfy desire, and the claims of right and duty which inhibit desire.

Although different schools of theory have tried to derive one from the other, they remain in some respects independent variables. Still another school of moralists has been impressed by the universality in conduct of actions which manifest approval and disapproval, praise and blame, sympathetic encouragement and resentment. Theorists of this school have been struck with the spontaneity and directness of such actions, since it is "natural," in the most immediate sense of the word, for men to show favor or disfavor toward the conduct of others. This is done without conscious reflection, without reference to the ideas of either a Good end which is to be attained or of a Duty which is authoritative. In fact, according to this school, the ideas of Good and Duty are secondary; the Good is that which calls out approbation; duties are derived from the pressure of others expressed in the rewards and penalties, in the praise and blame, they spontaneously attach to acts.

Upon this view, the problem of reflective morality is to discover the basis upon which men unconsciously manifest approval and resentment. In making explicit what is implicit in the spontaneous and direct attitudes of praise and blame, reflection introduces consistency and system into the reactions which take place without thought. It is significant that in morals the word "judgment" has a double sense. In respect to knowledge, the word has an intellectual sense. To judge is to weigh pros and cons in thought and decide according to the balance of evidence. This signification is the only one recognized in logical theory. But in human relations, it has a definitely practical meaning. To "judge" is to condemn or approve, praise or blame. Such judgments are practical reactions, not coldly intellectual propositions. They manifest favor and disfavor, and on account of the sensitiveness of persons to the likes and dislikes of others exercise a positive influence on those judged. The injunction in the New Testament "Judge not" is a familiar instance of this usage of judgment; it also indicates that indulgence in such judgments is itself a moral matter. The desire on one side to escape censure has a counterpart, as a motive of conduct, in a tendency to exhibit superiority by indulging in condemnation of others.

There is nothing more spontaneous, more "instinctive," than praise and blame of others. Reflective morality notes the inconsistency and arbitrary variations in popular expressions of esteem and disapproval, and seeks to discover a rational principle by which they will be justified and rendered coherent. It notes especially that unreflective acclaim and reproof merely repeat and reflect the scheme of values which is embodied in the social habits of a particular group. Thus a militant community admires and extols all warlike achievements and traits; an industrialized community sets store by thrift, calculation, constancy of labor, and applauds those persons who exhibit these qualities. In one group "success" signifies prowess; in the other group, the amassing of property; and praise and blame are correspondingly awarded. In Greek life, the contrast between the system of acts and dispositions prized by the Athenian and Spartan respectively was a stock theme of moralists. Recently, an analogous opposition has been set up by some critics between "Americanism" and "Europeanism."

These differences inevitably lead in time to asking a question: What plan of commendation and reprobation is to be itself approved and adopted? The question is the more acute because of the great influence of the attitude of others in shaping disposition. Habitual attitudes of favor and disfavor, often expressed in overt punishment and tangible reward and almost always in ridicule and conferring of prestige, are the weapons of customary morality. Moreover they are so deeply engrained in human nature, that, according to one view, the whole business of reflective morality and of moral theory is to determine a rational principle as the basis for their operation. The point may be illustrated by reference to the conceptions of virtue and vice. The theory in question holds that the morally good, as distinct from the good of satisfying desire, is the same as the virtuous; it holds that the right is also the virtuous, while the morally bad and the wrong are one with what is vicious. But the virtuous at first signifies that which is approved; the vicious that which is condemned. In customary morality, acts and traits of character are not esteemed because they are virtuous; rather they are virtues because they are supported by social approval and admiration. So virtue means valor in a martial society, and denotes enterprise, thrift, industriousness in an industrialized community, while it may signify poverty, rags, ascetic habits, in a community in which devotion to supernatural things is prized as the highest good. Reflection tries to reverse the order: it wants to discover what *should* be esteemed so that approbation will follow what is decided to be *worth* approving, instead of designating virtues on the basis of what happens to be especially looked up to and rewarded in a particular society.

§ 2. THE NATURE OF STANDARDS AND OF UTILITARIAN THEORY

The principle upon which the assignment of praise and blame rationally rests constitutes what is known as a *standard*. It is the foundation of judgment in its *practical* sense. In this type of theory the concept of Standard occupies the place held respectively by Good and Duty in the other theories already considered. The principle by which acclaim and reprehension should be regulated is made the dominant ethical "category," taking precedence of the good and the obligatory. For, on this theory, that which is morally good is that which is approved, while the right is that which should be approved. Duties pass from the mere *de facto* realm of things exacted by social pressure into the *de jure* realm of acts which are rightfully demanded only as they agree with the Standard of approval; otherwise they are coercive and are restrictive of freedom.   The right is that which *deserves* commendation; the wrong is that which *merits* punishment, overt or attenuated to the form of censure.

It is significant that, upon the whole, the idea of approval or disapproval and its proper standard is characteristic of English moral theory, as that of Ends is of Greek and Duty of Roman ethical philosophy.   It is implicit in Greek theory in the importance attached to measure and proportionateness in judging acts and in the tendency to identify *to agathon*, the good, with *to kalon*, the beautiful.   But in English moral theorizing the manifestation of commendation and condemnation, and their influence upon the formation of character, are for the first time made central.   It appears in Shaftesbury as an immediate intuition of moral sense, strictly comparable to "good taste" in esthetic matters; to Hume, approbation is identical with what "pleases on a *general* view," that is after reflective generalization in distinction from first and personal reaction; Adam Smith's conception that it is what satisfies the "*impartial* spectator" is a variant of the same notion.

To Bentham, most of the interpretations of his predecessors were still infected too much with "*ipse dixitism*," the vice, according to him, of all intuitional theories.   He sought for a general and impersonal, an objective, principle which should control and justify the personal reactions of good taste or whatever. In Smith and especially in Hume he found implicit the concept that the usefulness of a deed or a trait of character to others is the ultimate ground of approval, while disservice, harmfulness, is the ground of condemnation and depreciation. Men spontaneously applaud acts which help them, which further their happiness; no explanation has to be sought for this fact. Sympathy is also an original trait of human nature. Because of sympathy we praise acts which assist others even when our own fortunes are not involved; we are moved sympathetically to indignation by wilful infliction of suffering on third parties. Sympathy instinctively transports us to their position, and we share their glow of liking and their fire of resentment as if we were personally concerned. Only the abnormally callous are untouched emotionally by heroic acts of devotion to the welfare of others or by deeds of base ingratitude and malicious spite.

There are, however, definite limitations to the spontaneous and customary exercise of sympathetic admiration and resentment. It rarely extends beyond those near to us, members of our own family and our friends. It rarely operates with reference to those out of sight or to strangers, certainly not to enemies. In the second place, unreflective admiration and disesteem are superficial. They take account of striking, conspicuous cases of help and injury, but not those of a more delicate and subtle sort; they take notice of consequences in the way of assistance and harm which show themselves in a short time, but not those which emerge later, even though the latter are in truth the more important. And, finally, when certain acts have become thoroughly habitual, they are taken for granted like phenomena of nature and are not judged at all. The beneficial and hurtful consequences of laws and institutions, for example, are not taken into account by customary morality.

Hence follow certain changes introduced by the utilitarian theory of the standard of approbation. When men recognize that contribution to universal happiness or welfare is the only ground for admiration and esteem, they eliminate the three limitations just mentioned.   The standard is generalized; judgment must be passed upon consequences of weal and woe for *all* sentient creatures who are affected by an act.   The same emphasis upon general or widespread consequences, brings to the fore the idea of *equality*, and does it in a way which transforms the customary award of praise and blame, sympathy and resentment.   For the latter does not put the happiness of self and of others, of a member of the family and the outsider, of a fellow citizen and a stranger, of nobleman and commoner, of the lord and the peasant, of the man of distinction and the obscure person, of rich and poor, upon the same footing.   But the utilitarian theory, in addition to its insistence upon taking into consideration the widest, most general range of consequences, insists that in estimating consequences in the way of help and harm, pleasure and suffering, each one shall count as one, irrespective of distinctions of birth, sex, race, social status, economic and political position.   It is significant that the rise and chief influence of utilitarianism in England coincided socially with the manifestation of philanthropic sentiment on a large scale, and politically with the emergence of democratic ideals.[1]   'It is no accident that its chief practical influence was modification of the laws and institutions that sprang from and that fostered inequality.

§ 3. CONFUSION OF UTILITARIANISM WITH HEDONISM

So far we have passed by one important feature of utilitarianism.   We have spoken in general terms of welfare, of benefit and injury, with no attempt to specify in just what they consist.   Bentham, however, prided himself upon the fact that utilitarianism had a definite and measurable conception of

[1] The life of Bentham fell between 1748 and 1832; his chief disciple, John Stuart Mill, lived from 1806 to 1873.

their nature. They consist, according to him, of units of pleasure and pain, being merely their algebraic summation. Thus he reduced, according to his followers, the vague notion of welfare and happiness to a fact so precise as to be capable of quantitative statement.[1] This definition in terms of units of pleasure and pain had, however, another effect. It exposed utilitarianism to all the objections which can be brought against hedonism (see p. 208). Nor did the consequences of their identification stop at this point. It involved utilitarianism, as its critics promptly pointed out, in a peculiar contradiction. According to its conception of desire and of motive, the sole object and aim of all action is the obtaining of *personal* pleasure. The proper standard for judging the morality of action is, however, its contribution to the pleasure of *others*— the benefit conferred upon others than one's self. The utilitarians were thus faced by the problem of conflict between the strictly personal and selfish character of the motive of conduct, and the broadly social and philanthropic character of the standard of approval. Desire for private pleasure as the sole motive of action and universal benevolence as the principle of approval are at war with one another. The chief interest of Bentham was in the standard of judgment, and his acceptance of hedonistic psychology was, in the broad sense, an historic accident. He failed to realize the inconsistency of the two principles because his own interest was in the inequitable effect of the laws and institutions of his time upon the general distribution of happiness and unhappiness. He realized the extent to which they expressed class interests and were animated by favoritism to special interests, bringing benefit to the privileged few and harm and suffering to the masses. Now laws and institutions could be viewed *imper-*

[1] Thus Mill said: "He introduced into morals and politics those habits of thought, and modes of investigation, which are essential to the idea of science. . . . He, for the first time, introduced precision of thought in moral and political philosophy." *Autobiography*, pp. 65–67 of the *London edition of 1874*, and *Dissertations and Discussions*, " Essay on Bentham."

sonally, with respect only to their consequences, since motives cannot be attributed to laws and institutions as such.

His follower, John Stuart Mill, while interested in social and political reforms, was also interested in personal morality in a way in which Bentham was not. Therefore he brought the question of personal *disposition*, of *character*, to the fore, and instituted a transformation in utilitarian morals, although he never formally surrendered the hedonistic psychology. Before considering Mill's contribution in particular, however, we shall state the problem of the relation of disposition to beneficial social consequences in its general form. Suppose we drop the hedonistic emphasis upon states of pleasure and pain and substitute the wider, if vaguer, idea of well-being, welfare, happiness, as the proper standard of approval. The problem of the relation of the standard to personal disposition still remains. The moral problem which confronts every person is how regard for general welfare, for happiness of others than himself, is to be made a regulative purpose in his conduct. It is difficult to make a regard for general happiness the standard of right and wrong, even in a purely theoretical estimate. For such a method of appraisal goes contrary to our natural tendency to put first our own happiness and that of persons near to us. This difficulty, however, is slight in comparison with that of making the intellectual estimate effective in action whenever it conflicts with our natural partiality in our own favor.

It is evident that only intimate personal disposition will enable us to solve these problems. The more importance we attach to objective consequences as the standard, the more we are compelled to fall back upon personal character as the only guarantee that this standard will operate, either intellectually in our estimates or practically in our behavior. The alleged precision for which Bentham was praised introduces an impossibility into actual conduct. One can make an estimate on the basis of experience of the general tendency of a proposed action upon welfare and suffering; no one can figure out in advance all the units of pleasure and pain (even admitting they can be reduced to unit quantities) which will follow. We are sure that the *attitude* of personal kindliness, of sincerity and fairness, will make our judgment of the effects of a proposed action on the good of others infinitely more likely to be correct than will those of hate, hypocrisy, and self-seeking. A man who trusted simply to details of external consequences might readily convince himself that the removal of a certain person by murder would contribute to general happiness. One cannot imagine an honest person convincing himself that a disposition of disregard for human life would have beneficial consequences.   It is true, on one hand, that the ultimate standard for judgment of acts is their objective consequences; the outcome constitutes the meaning of an act.   But it is equally true that the warrant for correctness of judgment and for power of judgment to operate as an influence in conduct lies in the intrinsic make-up of character; it would be safer to trust a man of a kind and honest disposition without much ability in calculation than it would a man having great power of foresight of the future who was malicious and insincere.   When, on the other hand, we are judging the moral value of laws and institutions (that is to say, estimating them from the standpoint of their bearing upon the general welfare), impersonal and minute consideration of consequences is in order, since they, being impersonal, have no inner disposition one way or another.

Mill accordingly brought utilitarianism in closer accord with the unbiased moral sense of mankind when he said that "to do as you would be done by and to love your neighbor as yourself, constitute the ideal perfection of utilitarian morality." For such a statement puts disposition, character, first, and calculation of specific results second.   Consequently on Mill's view we can say that "laws and social arrangements should place the happiness of every individual as nearly as possible

in harmony with the interest of the whole, and that education and opinion, which have so vast a power over human
character should so use that power as to establish in the mind
of every individual an indissoluble association between his
own happiness and the good of the whole." In short, we have
a principle by which to judge the moral value of social arrangements: Do they tend to lead members of the community to
find their happiness in the objects and purposes which bring
happiness to others? There is also an ideal provided for the
processes of education, formal and informal. Education should
create an interest in all persons in furthering the general good,
so that they will find their own happiness realized in what they
can do to improve the conditions of others.

Emphasis upon personal disposition also appears in Mill's
desire to see certain attitudes cultivated in and for themselves,
as if they were ends in themselves without conscious thought
of their external consequences. Intrinsically, and by our very
make-up, apart from any calculation, we prize friendly relations with others. We naturally

"desire to be in unity with our fellow creatures. . . . The social
state is at once so natural, so necessary, and so habitual to man,
that except in some unusual circumstances or by an effort of voluntary abstraction, *he never conceives himself otherwise than as a
member of a body.* . . . Any condition, therefore, which is essential to a state of society becomes more and more an inseparable
part of every person's conception of the state of things he is born
into and which is the destiny of a human being." This strengthening
of social ties leads the individual "to identify his *feelings* more
and more with the good" of others. "He comes, as though instinctively, to be conscious of himself as a being, who, *of course*,
pays regard to others. The good of others becomes to him a thing
naturally and necessarily to be attended to, like any of the physical conditions of our existence." This social feeling, finally, however weak, does not present itself "as a superstition of education,
or a law despotically imposed from without, but as an attribute
which it would not be well to be without. . . . Few but those

whose mind is a moral blank could *bear* to lay out their course of life on the line of paying no regard to others except so far as their own private interests compels." [1]

Even under the head of sympathy, Bentham's

"recognition does not extend to the more complex forms of the feeling—the love of *loving*, the need of a sympathizing support, or of an object of admiration and reverence." [2] "Self culture, the training by the human being himself of his affections and will . . . is a blank in Bentham's system. The other and co-equal part, the regulation of his outward actions, must be altogether halting and imperfect without the first; for how can we judge in what manner many an action will affect the worldly interests of ourselves or others unless we take in, as part of the question, its influence on the regulation of our or their affections and desires?" [3]

In other words, Mill saw that a weakness of Bentham's theory lay in his supposing that the factors which make up disposition are of value only as moving us to special acts which produce pleasure; to Mill they have a worth of their own as *direct* sources and ingredients of happiness. So Mill says:

"I regard any considerable increase of human happiness, through mere changes in outward circumstances, unaccompanied by changes in the state of desires, as hopeless." [4] And in his *Autobiography*, speaking of his first reaction against Benthamism, he says: "I, for the first time, gave its proper place, among the prime necessities of human well-being, to the internal culture of the individual. I ceased to attach almost exclusive importance to the ordering of outward circumstances. . . . The cultivation of the feelings became one of the cardinal points in my ethical and philosophical creed." [5]

[1] *Utilitarianism*, ch. iii., *passim*.
[2] *Early Essays*, p. 354. (Reprint by Gibbs, London, 1897.)
[3] *Ibid.*, p. 357.
[4] *Ibid.*, p. 404.
[5] *Autobiography*, London, 1884, p. 143.

The close connection between happiness and traits of character is also borne out by the fact that pleasures differ in *quality*, and not merely in quantity and intensity. Appreciation of poetry, of art, of science yields a kind of satisfaction which is not to be compared with that coming from purely sensuous sources. The extent to which the working standard is shifted by Mill from pleasures to character (since the quality of pleasure is ranked by the nature of the personal trait the pleasure accompanies) is obvious in the following quotation: "No intelligent person would consent to be a fool, no instructed person would be an ignoramus, no person of feeling and conscience would be selfish and base, even though they should be persuaded that the fool, the dunce or the rascal is better satisfied with his lot than they are. . . . It is better to be a human being dissatisfied than a pig satisfied."

We have devoted considerable space to a consideration of the shift from Bentham to Mill, not so much as a matter of historical contrast and information as because the position of the latter involves in fact, although Mill never quite acknowledges it in words, a surrender of the hedonistic element in utilitarianism. Since this hedonistic element is that which renders utilitarianism vulnerable in theory and unworkable in practice, it is significant to know that the conception of regard for social (that is widespread and impartially measured) welfare may be maintained as a standard of approbation in spite of historic utilitarianism's entanglement with an untenable hedonism. This revised version recognizes the great part played by factors internal to the self in creating a worthy happiness, while it also provides a standard for the moral appraisal of laws and institutions. For aside from the direct suffering which bad social arrangements occasion, they have a deteriorating effect upon those dispositions which conduce to an elevated and pure happiness.

Institutions are good not only because of their direct contribution to well-being but even more because they favor the development of the worthy dispositions from which issue noble enjoyments.

§ 4. THE RELATION OF ENDS AND STANDARDS

Purposes, aims, ends-in-view, are distinct from standards and yet are closely related to them; and *vice versa*. Ends-in-view are connected with desire; they look to the future, because they are projections of the objects in which desires would be satisfied. Standards, on the other hand, envisage acts already performed or viewed in imagination *as if* they had been performed. An object viewed as an end or fulfillment of desire is good in proportion as it is found to be a genuine satisfaction or realization of desire. From the standpoint of a standard, an act is good if it can evoke and sustain *approbation*. At the outset, the approbation in question is that proceeding from others. Will the group, or some particular influential member of the group, tolerate, abet, encourage, praise me if I act thus and so? The admiration and resentment of others is the mirror in which one beholds the moral quality of his act reflected back to him. Because of this reflection the agent can judge his act from a standpoint which is different from that of a satisfaction directly promised. He is led to widen and generalize his conception of his act when he takes into account the reaction of others; he views his act objectively when he takes the standpoint of standard; personally, when it is an end merely as such.

Later on, the thought of the reaction of favor or disfavor of a particular social group or a particular person tends to recede to the background. An *ideal* spectator is projected and the doer of the act looks at his proposed act through the eyes of this impartial and far-seeing objective judge. Although end and standard are two distinct conceptions having different meanings, yet it is the very nature of a standard to demand that what is approvable according to it shall *become* an end. In other words, it calls for the creation of a new end; or, in case the end suggested by desire is approved, for an end with a new quality, that of having received the stamp of approval. Unless the conception of standard arose from a different source and had a different meaning from that of ends, it could not exercise a controlling formative influence on the latter. The significance of the standard is that it involves a conception of the *way* in which ends that are adopted *should* be formed; namely, that they should be such as to merit approbation because their execution will conduce to the general well-being.

Recognition of this fact enables us to deal with a problem which is attended with a good deal of difficulty. The problem is illustrated in the so-called hedonistic paradox, that the way to attain pleasure is not to seek for it. And this saying may be paralleled by another paradox, namely, that the way to achieve virtue is not to aim directly at it. For the standard is not the same as the end of desire. Hence contribution to the general good may be the standard of reflective approval without its being the end-in-view. Indeed, it is hard to imagine its being made the end of desire; as a direct object to be aimed at, it would be so indeterminate and vague that it would only arouse a diffused sentimental state, without indicating just how and where conduct should be directed. Desire on the other hand points to a definite and concrete object at which to aim. After this end has occurred to the mind it is examined and tested from another point of view: Would the action which achieves it further the well-being of all concerned?

The idea of happiness is originally derived from cases of fulfilled desire. It is a general term for the fact that while desires are different and the objects which satisfy them are different, there is one common quality in all of them: namely, the fact of being fulfillments. This is a formal trait. It is a mistake to suppose that there is homogeneity of material or content, just because there is the single name "happiness." One might as well suppose that all persons named Smith are just alike because they have the same name. No two concrete cases of happiness are just like each other in actual stuff and make-up. They are alike in being cases of fulfillment, of meeting the requirements set up by some desire. A miser finds satisfaction in storing up money, and a liberal person in spending it to give happiness to others. One man is happy when he gets ahead of others in some tangible way and another man is happy when he helps others out of some trouble. In material content, the two cases differ radically; in form they are alike, since both occupy the same status and play the same rôle—that of satisfying a desire.

The function of the standard then is to discriminate between the various material kinds of satisfaction so as to determine which kind of happiness is truly moral; that is, approvable. It says that among the different kinds that one is to be approved which at the same time brings satisfaction to others, or which at least harmonizes with their well-being in that it does not inflict suffering upon them. It does not tell what things should be specifically aimed at. It does tell us how to proceed in passing condemnation or giving approval to those ends and purposes which occur to the mind independently because of our desires. When this point is clearly recognized, we can appreciate the artificial nature of a problem which is often raised. It has been asserted that the crux of all moral theory is the relation between personal happiness and general happiness. It is asserted that morality as justice requires that there be a complete equation between the two; that we cannot be morally satisfied with a world in which the conduct which brings good to others brings suffering to the one who promotes the interests of others, or in which the conduct which makes others suffer yields happiness to the one who injures others. Much ingenuity has been spent in explaining away the frequent discrepancies. For it may even be argued that although extreme egoistic isolation is unfavorable to happiness, so also are great breadth and sensitiveness of affections; that the person who stands the best show of being happy is the one who exercises a prudent control over his sympathies, and so keeps from getting involved in the fortunes of other persons. If we once become aware of the difference between the standard and end, this problem of instituting an identity or equation between personal and general happiness is seen to be unreal. The standard says that we should desire those objects and find our satisfactions in the things which also bring good to those with whom we are associated, in friendship, comradeship, citizenship, the pursuit of science, art, and so on.

Many an individual solves the problem. He does so not by any theoretical demonstration that what gives others happiness will also make him happy, but by voluntary choice of those objects which do bring good to others. He gets a personal satisfaction or happiness because his desire is fulfilled, but his desire has first been made after a definite pattern. This enjoyment may be shorter in duration and less intense than those which he might have had some other way. But it has one mark which is unique and which for that individual may outweigh everything else. He has achieved a happiness which has *approved* itself to him, and this quality of being an approved happiness may render it invaluable, not to be compared with others. By personal choice among the ends suggested by desires of objects which are in agreement with the needs of social relations, an individual achieves a *kind* of happiness which is harmonious with the happiness of others. This is the only sense in which there is an equation between personal and general happiness. But it is also the only sense which is morally required.

§ 5. THE PLACE OF JUSTICE AND BENEVOLENCE IN THE STANDARD

When contribution to a shared good is taken to be the standard of approbation, a question comes up as to the relation of justice to the standard. At first sight, it seems as if benevo-

lence were exalted to such a point that justice almost falls out of
the moral picture. At all events, this conception of the nature
of the standard has been attacked on the ground that justice
is the supreme virtue and that the standard of general well-
being subordinates justice, said to be self-sufficing in isolation,
to something beyond itself in the way of consequences. Fundamentally, the issue here is that which we have considered
previously in other guises: namely, the place of consequences
in moral conduct. Those who regard consideration of consequences to be a degradation of morals take their stand on some
abstract principle of justice. *"Fiat justitia, ruat coelum"*
is the classic expression of this point of view. Let justice be
done, be the consequences what they may, even to the collapse
of the heavens. It is argued that regard for consequences,
even such consequences as the common and shared good,
reduces justice to a matter of expediency and abates its authority and majesty.

The reply to this objection is twofold. In the first place,
elimination from the moral standard of the consequences of
actions leaves us with only a formal principle; it sets up an
abstraction and treats morality as mere conformity to an
abstraction instead of as vital effort in behalf of a significant
end. Experience shows that the subordination of human good
to an external and formal rule tends in the direction of harshness and cruelty. The common saying that justice should be
tempered with mercy is the popular way of stating recognition
of the hard and ultimately *unjust* character of setting up a
principle of action which is divorced from all consideration of
human consequences. Justice as an end in itself is a case of
making an idol out of a means at the expense of the end which
the means serves. The second factor in the reply to the objection is that justice is not an external means to human welfare
but a means which is organically integrated with the end it
serves. There are means which are constituent parts of the
consequences they bring into being, as tones are integral

constituents of music as well as means to its production, and as food is an indispensable ingredient within the organism which it serves. On this account the character, the self, which has adopted fair play and equity into its own attitude will not only have the sense of humanity which protects it from harsh application of the principle, but will also be protected from any temptation to disregard the principle in order to obtain some short-term specific good. A rough analogy of what is here signified is that while rules of the hygiene of eating grow out of the service which foods render to the well-being of the organism, and are not abstract ends on their own account, yet nevertheless these rules, when once understood in their relation to the end they serve, save us from using food as a mere means to a temporary enjoyment. We can fall back on the rule in case of doubt.

There is moreover an inherent difficulty in the conception that justice can be separated from the effect of actions and attitudes upon human well-being. The separation leaves the practical meaning of standard arbitrary or open to different constructions. It is sometimes interpreted to signify strict retribution, an eye for an eye, a tooth for a tooth. Herbert Spencer gives another meaning to the principle, and employs this meaning to justify a thoroughgoing policy of *laissez faire* in social matters. He identifies the principle of justice with the relation of cause and effect in its biological meaning, that is with natural selection and the elimination of the unfit in the struggle for existence. It is "just" he asserts that the inferior should stand the consequences of their inferiority and that the superior should reap the rewards of their superiority. To interfere with the workings of natural selection is thus to violate the law of justice. In other words, Spencer uses the abstract principle of justice to warrant a policy of extreme individualism in letting the "natural" play of self-interest in a competitive society take its course. Examples of other interpretations of justice might be given.

But the two instances cited should indicate the complete falsity of the common notion that justice carries its definite meaning. The truth lies on the other side. The meaning of justice in concrete cases is something to be determined by seeing what consequences will bring about human welfare in a fair and even way.

Another type of objection to social welfare as the standard of approval is that it elevates sentimentality to a supreme position in morals. Thus Carlyle condemned utilitarianism as "a universal syllabus of sentimental twaddle." It is true that there is a close relation between the standard of extensive well-being and the attitude of sympathy. But regard for consequences does not encourage giving away to every sentiment of pity and sympathy which is experienced. On the contrary, it says that we should restrain acting upon them until we have considered what the effect will be on human happiness if we give way to them. The emotion of sympathy is morally invaluable. But it functions properly when used as a principle of reflection and insight, rather than of direct action. Intelligent sympathy widens and deepens concern for consequences. To put ourselves in the place of another, to see things from the standpoint of his aims and values, to humble our estimate of our own pretensions to the level they assume in the eyes of an impartial observer, is the surest way to appreciate what justice demands in concrete cases. The real defect of sentimentalism is that it fails to consider the consequences of acting upon objective well-being; it makes the immediate indulgence of a dominant emotion more important than results.

The tendency, moreover, of adopting social well-being as a standard is to make us intellectually sensitive and critical about the effect of laws, social arrangements, and education upon human happiness and development. Historic utilitarianism, even with the handicap of its hedonistic psychology, did a great work in Great Britain in getting rid of inequalities in law and administration, and in making the mass of men conscious of the connection which exists between political oppression and corruption on one side and the suffering of the masses on the other.

The meaning to be given, from the moral point of view, to the idea of reform and the reformer furnishes a good test of the standard of approval.   In one meaning, reform is almost synonymous with officious meddling; with an assumption that the would-be reformers know better than others what is good for them and can proceed to confer some great boon upon them. But the true significance of "the greatest good of the greatest number" is that social conditions should be such that all individuals can exercise their own initiative in a social medium which will develop their personal capacities and reward their efforts. That is, it is concerned with providing the objective political, economic, and social conditions which will enable the greatest possible number because of their *own* endeavors to have a full and generous share in the values of living. Of course direct help to others is needed in times of illness, physical incapacity, pecuniary distress, etc. But the chief application of the standard is concern for the influence of objective social conditions.   Thus the standard saves endeavors at social change, made in its name, from the offensiveness of snobbery and personal interference.   It accomplishes beneficent ends by the means of impersonal justice.

The opposition which is frequently instituted between beneficence and justice rests upon a narrow conception of the latter as well as upon a sentimental conception of the former. If beneficence is taken to signify acts which exceed the necessities of legal obligation, and justice to denote the strict letter of moral law there is, of course, a wide gap between them. But in reality the scope of justice is broad enough to cover all the conditions which make for social welfare, while a large part of what passes as charity and philanthropy is merely a makeshift to compensate for lack of just social conditions.

The classic conception of justice is derived from Roman law, and shares its formal legalistic character. It is "rendering to another that which is his." According to the legal conception of what belongs to a man, the idea is limited to rather external matters, material property, repute and honor, esteem for good character, etc. But in its wide meaning the formula only raises a question, instead of affording a solution. What does belong to a man as man? How is what is morally due to a man to be measured? Can it be fixed by conventional considerations? Or is what is owed to a person anything less than opportunity to become all which he is capable of becoming? Suppose a man is detected in violation of the social code. Is what is owed him in the way of justice some retributive penalty, as exactly proportioned as possible to his offense, on the principle of an eye for an eye, a tooth for a tooth? or is it the treatment which will tend to evoke his own efforts at moral betterment? Is "justice" to be measured on the ground of existing social status, or on the ground of possibilities of development? Such questions suggest that social utilitarianism, when freed from its hedonistic handicap, makes justice to be a concern for the objective conditions of personal growth and achievement which cannot be distinguished from beneficence in its fundamental and objective sense.

§ 6.   PRAISE AND BLAME AS MORAL FORCES

It was noted earlier in passing (p. 27) that the concept of virtue is closely connected with the operation of approbation. It is not too much to say of primitive morals that in them traits of character are not approved because they are virtuous, but are virtuous because they are approved, while whatever is generally censured is *ipso facto*, regarded as vicious. Reflective morality reverses this attitude. It is concerned to discover what traits of character should be approved; it identifies virtue not with that which is *de facto* approved but that which is approv*able*, which *should* be approved. But, as we have often had occasion to note, a large strain of customary morality holds over in morality which is theoretically reflective. "Conventional morality" is precisely a morality of praise and blame based on the code of valuations which happens to be current at a particular time in a particular social group. Whatever conforms, at least outwardly, to current practices, especially those of an institutional sort, receives commendation or at least passes without censure; whatever deviates exposes one to censure. The practical effect is a negative morality; virtue is identified with "respectability," and respectability means such conduct as is exempt from overt reproach and censure rather than what is inherently *worthy* of respect. The moral ideal of multitudes of persons comes to be that sort of behavior which will pass without arousing adverse comment, just as a child too often identifies the "right" with whatever passes without a scolding.

Accordingly, this is a convenient place in which to consider the point we passed over at first, namely, the proper moral place and function of praise and blame.

At first sight, it might seem as if reflection on the customary use of approbation and condemnation would still leave praise and blame as primary factors, only giving them a standard by which to operate. Such is not the case, however. Reflection reacts to modify the character and use of praise and blame. The latter tend to fix the attention of the one commended or reprobated upon the way in which he can secure the one and avoid the other. Their effect therefore is to distract attention from the reasons and causes which make conduct praise*worthy* and blame*worthy*. Habitual exposure to praise and blame makes one think of how he may exculpate himself from accusation and may recommend himself to favor. Morality that makes much of blaming breeds a defensive and apologetic attitude; the person subjected to it thinks up excuses instead of thinking what objects are worthy to be pursued. Moreover, it distracts attention from thought of objective conditions and causes, because it tends to make one want to get even for being blamed by passing the blame on to others. One relieves himself from a charge by transferring it to some one else. In stronger natures, resentment is produced and to a point where the person blamed feels he is doing a brave thing in defying all authority. In others, it produces a feeling which put in words amounts to: "What is the use? It makes no difference what I do, since I get blamed anyway."

Reflective morality instead of leaving praise and blame where they were except for putting under them a rational basis tends to shift the emphasis to scrutiny of conduct in an objective way, that is with reference to its causes and results. What is desirable is that a person shall see for himself what he is doing and why he is doing it; shall be sensitive to results in fact and in anticipation, and shall be able to analyze the forces which make him act as he does act. Accordingly, approval and disapproval themselves are subjected to judgment by a standard instead of being taken as ultimate. On the whole, the prevalence of a morality based on praise and blame is evidence of the extent to which customary and conventional forces still influence a morality nominally reflective. The possession of a reflective standard checks and directs the use of praise and blame as it does the use of other human tendencies. It makes men realize that reward and punishment, commendation and condemnation are good or bad according to their consequences and that they may be used immorally as well as helpfully.

We have already noted the reflex origin of the traits regarded as virtuous and vicious. They are derived at the outset from the conceptions of merit and demerit, of deserts; and meritoriousness, deservingness, is measured by the reactions of others. It is others who, approving and disapproving, award honor, esteem, merit. For this reason, as has also been noted, virtues and vices in morals as far as dominated by custom are strictly correlative to the ruling institutions and habits of a given social group. Its members are trained to commend and admire whatever conforms to its established ways of life; hence the great divergence of schemes of valuation of conduct in different civilizations. Their common element is formal rather than material—namely, adherence to prevailing customs. *Nomos* is indeed "king of all," and especially of acts and traits of character deemed virtues and vices.

The attempt to discover a *standard* upon the basis of which approbation and disapprobation, esteem and disteem, *should* be awarded has therefore nothing less than a revolutionary effect upon the whole concept of virtue and vice. For it involves *criticism* of prevailing habits of valuation. The very idea of a standard is *intellectual;* it implies something universally applicable. It does not eliminate the element of favor and hostility to certain modes of conduct. But it introduces the regulation of these manifestations by something beyond themselves. Customary morals naturally "make it hot" for those who transgress its code, and make it comfortable for those who conform. The reflective standard holds individuals to responsibility for the ways in which favor and dislike are expressed. It makes prominent the fact that in judging, in commending and condemning, we are judging ourselves, revealing our own tastes and desires. Approval and disapproval, the attitude of attributing vice and virtue, becomes itself a vice or a virtue according to the way in which it is administered.

§ 7. THE CONCEPTION OF VIRTUE IN REFLECTIVE MORALITY

In customary morality it is possible to draw up a list or catalogue of vices and virtues. For the latter reflect some definite existing custom, and the former some deviation from or violation of custom. The acts approved and disapproved have therefore the same definiteness and fixity as belong to the customs to which they refer. In reflective morality, a list of virtues has a much more tentative status. Chastity, kindness, honesty, patriotism, modesty, toleration, bravery, etc., cannot be given a fixed meaning, because each expresses an interest in objects and institutions which are changing. In form, *as* interests, they may be permanent, since no community could endure in which there were not, say, fair dealing, public spirit, regard for life, faithfulness to others. But no two communities conceive the objects to which these qualities attach in quite identical ways. They can be defined, therefore, only on the basis of *qualities characteristic of interest*, not on the basis of permanent and uniform objects in which interest is taken. This is as true of, say, temperance and chastity as it is of regard for life, which in some communities does not extend to girl babies nor to the aged, and which in all historic communities is limited by war with hostile communities.

Accordingly we shall discuss virtue through enumeration of traits which must belong to an attitude if it is to be genuinely an interest, not by an enumeration of virtues as if they were separate entities. (1) *An interest must be wholehearted.* Virtue is integrity, vice is duplicity. Sincerity is another name for the same quality, for it signifies that devotion to an object is unmixed and undiluted. The quality has a much broader scope than might at first seem to be the case.

Conscious hypocrisy is rare. Divided and inconsistent interest is common. Devotion that is complete, knowing no reservations and exceptions, is extremely difficult to attain. We imagine we are whole-hearted when we throw ourselves into a line of action which is agreeable, failing to notice that we give up or act upon an incompatible interest when obstacles arise. Whole-heartedness is something quite different from immediate enthusiasm and ardor. It always has an emotional quality, but it is far from being identical with a succession of even intense emotional likings for a succession of things into each of which we eagerly throw ourselves. For it requires consistency, continuity, and community of purpose and effort. And this condition cannot be fulfilled except

when the various objects and ends which succeed one another have been brought into order and unity by reflection
upon the nature and bearing of each one.   We cannot be
genuinely whole-hearted unless we are single-minded.

Hence (2) the interest which constitutes a disposition virtuous must be continuous and *persistent.* One swallow does
not make a summer nor does a passing right interest, no matter how strong, constitute a virtue.   Fair weather "virtue"
has a bad name because it indicates lack of stability. It demands character to stick it out when conditions are adverse,
as they are when there is danger of incurring the ill-will of
others, or when it requires more than ordinary energy to
overcome obstacles.   The *vitality* of interest in what is reflectively approved is attested by persistence under unfavorable conditions.

A complete interest must be (3) *impartial* as well as enduring.   Interest, apart from a character formed and forti-
fied through reflection, is partial, and in that sense divided and,
though unconsciously, insincere. A person readily tends to
evince interest in the well-being of friends and members of his
family, and to be indifferent to those with whom he is not
bound by ties of gratitude or affection. It is easy to have one
scale for determining interest in those of one's own nation
and a totally different one for the regard of those of another
race, color, religion, or nationality.   Complete universality
of interest is, of course, impossible in the sense of equality of
strength or force of quantity; that is, it would be mere pretense to suppose that one can be as *much* interested in those
at a distance with whom one has little contact as in those
with whom one is in constant communication. But equity,
or impartiality, of interest is a matter of quality not of quantity as in-iquity is a matter not of more or less, but of using
uneven measures of judgment. Equity demands that *when* one
has to act in relation to others, no matter whether friends or
strangers, fellow citizens or foreigners, one should have an equal

and even measure of value as far as the interests of the others come into the reckoning. In an immediate or emotional sense it is not possible to love our enemies as we love our friends. But the maxim to love our enemies as we love ourselves signifies that in our conduct we should take into account their interests at the same rate of estimate as we rate our own. It is a principle for regulating judgment of the bearings of our acts on the happiness of others.

Single-mindedness of purpose would be narrow were it not united to breadth and impartiality of interest. The conception that virtue resides in fundamental and thoroughgoing interest in approved objects accomplishes more than merely saving us from the identification of virtues with whatever is conventionally and currently prized in a particular community or social set. For it protects us from an unreal separation of virtuous qualities from one another. The mere idea of a catalogue of different virtues commits us to the notion that virtues may be kept apart, pigeon-holed in water-tight compartments. In fact virtuous traits interpenetrate one another; this unity is involved in the very idea of integrity of character. At one time persistence and endurance in the face of obstacles is the most prominent feature; then the attitude is the excellence called courage. At another time, the trait of impartiality and equity is uppermost, and we call it justice. At other times, the necessity for subordinating immediate satisfaction of a strong appetite or desire to a comprehensive good is the conspicuous feature. Then the disposition is denominated temperance, self-control. When the prominent phase is the need for thoughtfulness, for consecutive and persistent attention, in order that these other qualities may function, the interest receives the name of moral wisdom, insight, conscientiousness. In each case the difference is one of emphasis only.

This fact is of practical as well as theoretical import. The supposition that virtues are separated from one another leads, when it is acted upon, to that narrowing and hardening of action which induces many persons to conceive of all morality as negative and restrictive. When, for example, an independent thing is made of temperance or self-control it becomes mere inhibition, a sour constraint. But as one phase of an interpenetrated whole, it is the positive harmony characteristic of integrated interest. Is justice thought of as an isolated virtue? Then it takes on a mechanical and quantitative form, like the exact meting out of praise and blame, reward and punishment. Or it is thought of as vindication of abstract and impersonal law—an attitude which always tends to make men vindictive and leads them to justify their harshness as a virtue. To the notion of courage there still adheres something of its original notion of fortitude in meeting an enemy. The Greeks broadened the conception to include all the disagreeable things which need to be borne but which one would like to run away from. As soon as we recognize that there can be no continuity in maintaining and executing a purpose which does not at some time meet difficulties and obstacles that are disagreeable, we also recognize that courage is no separate thing. Its scope is as wide as the fullness of positive interest which causes us in spite of difficulties to seek for the realization of the object to which the interest is attached. Otherwise it shrinks to mere stoical and negative resistance, a passive rather than an active virtue.

Finally, conscientiousness is sometimes treated as if it were mere morbid anxiety about the state of one's own virtue. It may even become a kind of sublimated egoism, since the person concentrates his thoughts upon himself, none the less egoistic because concerned with personal "goodness" instead of with personal pleasure or profit. In other cases, it becomes a kind of anxious scrupulosity which is so fearful of going wrong that it abstains as much as possible from positive outgoing action. Concern for the good is reduced to a paralyzing solicitude to be preserved from falling into error.

Energy that should go into action is absorbed in prying into motives. Conscience, moral thoughtfulness, makes us cowards as soon as it is isolated from courage.

Another bad consequence of treating virtues as if they were separate from one another and capable of being listed one by one is the attempt to cultivate each one by itself, instead of developing a rounded and positive character. There are, however, in traditional teachings many reminders of the wholeness of virtue. One such saying is that "love is the fulfilling of the law." For in its ethical sense, love signifies completeness of devotion to the objects esteemed good. Such an interest, or love, is marked by temperance because a comprehensive interest demands a harmony which can be attained only by subordination of particular impulses and passions. It involves courage because an active and genuine interest nerves us to meet and overcome the obstacles which stand in the way of its realization. It includes wisdom or thoughtfulness because sympathy, concern for the welfare of all affected by conduct, is the surest guarantee for the exercise of *consideration*, for examination of a proposed line of conduct in all its bearings. And such a complete interest is the only way in which justice can be assured. For it includes as part of itself impartial concern for all conditions which affect the common welfare, be they specific acts, laws, economic arrangements, political institutions, or whatever.

In the case of both the Good and Duty, we noted the moral effect of different social environments. The principle applies equally (and perhaps more obviously) to the use made of approval in determining standards as tests of conduct and the appraisal of virtues and vices. As we have had occasion to observe, each community tends to approve that which is in line with what it prizes in practice. Theoretical approvals that run counter to strong social tendencies tend to become purely nominal. In theory and in verbal instruction our present society is the heir of a great idealistic tradition. Through religion and from other sources, love of neighbor, exact equity, kindliness of action and judgment, are taught and in theory accepted. The structure of society, however, puts emphasis upon other qualities. "Business" absorbs a large part of the life of most persons and business is conducted upon the basis of ruthless competition for private gain. National life is organized on the basis of exclusiveness and tends to generate suspicion, fear, often hatred, of other peoples. The world is divided into classes and races, and, in spite of acceptance of an opposed theory, the standards of valuation are based on the class, race, color, with which one identifies oneself. The convictions that obtain in personal morality are negated on a large scale in collective conduct, and for this reason are weakened even in their strictly personal application. They cannot be made good in practice except as they are extended to include the remaking of the social environment, economic, political, international.

LITERATURE

The literature on utilitarianism is voluminous. For its history, see Albee, *History of Utilitarianism*, 1902; Stephen, *The English Utilitarians*, three vols., 1900; Halévy, *La Formation du Radicalisme philosophique*, Vols. I. and II.

Criticisms of it will be found in the references on hedonism at the close of Chapter II. Expositions and criticisms are found also in Lecky, *History of European Morals*, 3rd ed., 1916; Stephen, *Science of Ethics*, 1882, chs. iv. and v.; Höffding, *Ethik*, 1888, ch. vii.; Grote, *Examination of the Utilitarian Morals;* Wilson and Fowler, *Principles of Morals*, Vol. I., pp. 98–112; Vol. II., pp. 262–273; Green, *Prolegomena to Ethics*, 1890, pp. 240–255, 399–415; Sidgwick, *The Ethics of T. H. Green, Herbert Spencer and J. Martineau*, 1902. His *Methods of Ethics*, 1901, almost throughout a critical examination and exposition of utilitarianism; Sharp, *Ethics*, 1928, ch. xvii.; Everett, *Moral Values*, 1918, ch. v.

Upon the principle of virtue in general, see Plato, *Republic*, 427–443; Aristotle, *Ethics*, Books II. and IV.; Kant, *Theory of Ethics*, trans. by Abbott, pp. 164–182, 305, 316–322; Green, *Prolegomena*, pp. 256–314 (and for conscientiousness, pp. 323–337); Paulsen, *System of Ethics*, 1899, pp. 475–482; Alexander, *Moral Order and Progress*, pp. 242–253; Stephen, *Science of Ethics*, 1882, ch. v.; Spencer, *Principles of Ethics*, Vol. II., pp. 3–34 and 263–276; Sidgwick, *Methods of Ethics*, 1901, pp. 2–5 and 9–10; Rickaby, *Aquinas Ethicus*, Vol. I., pp. 155–195; Fite, *Moral Philosophy*, 1925, ch. iii., contains a discussion of variations in popular standards.

For natural ability and virtue: Hume, *Treatise*, Part II., Book III., and *Inquiry*, Appendix IV.; Bonar, *Intellectual Virtues*.

For discussions of special virtues: Aristotle, *Ethics*, Book III., and Book VII., chs. i.–x.; for justice: Aristotle, *Ethics*, Book V.; Rickaby, *Moral Philosophy*, pp. 102–108, and *Aquinas Ethicus* (see Index); Paulsen, *System of Ethics*, 1899, pp. 599–637; Mill, *Utilitarianism*, ch. v.; Sidgwick, *Methods of Ethics*, 1901, Book III., ch. v., and see Index; also criticism of Spencer in his *Lectures on the Ethics of Green, Spencer and Martineau*, 1902, pp. 272–302; Spencer, *Principles of Ethics*, Vol. II.; Stephen, *Science of Ethics*, 1882, ch. v.

For benevolence, see Aristotle, *Ethics*, Books VII.–IX. (on friendship); Rickaby, *Moral Philosophy*, pp. 237–244, and *Aquinas Ethicus* (see charity and almsgiving in Index); Paulsen, *System*, 1899, chs. viii. and x. of Part III.; Sidgwick, *Methods of Ethics*, 1901, Book II., ch. iv.; Spencer, *Principles of Ethics*, Vol. II.; see also the references under sympathy and altruism at end of Chapter XV.

On JUSTICE, Spencer, *Principles of Ethics*, Part IV.; Hobhouse, *The Elements of Social Justice*, 1922; Tufts, "Some Contributions of Psychology to the Conception of Justice," *Philosophical Review*, Vol. XV., p. 361; Calkins, *The Good Man and the Good*, 1918, ch. x.

CHAPTER V

MORAL JUDGMENT AND KNOWLEDGE

§ 1. MORAL JUDGMENTS AS INTUITIVE OR DEVELOPED

THAT reflective morality, since it *is* reflective, involves thought, and knowledge is a truism. The truism raises, however, important problems of theory. What is the nature of knowledge in its moral sense? What is its function? How does it originate and operate? To these questions, writers upon morals have given different answers. Those, for example, who have dwelt upon approval and resentment as the fundamental ethical factor have emphasized its spontaneous and "instinctive" character—that is, its non-reflective nature— and have assigned a subordinate position to the intellectual factor in morals. Those who, like Kant, have made the authority of duty supreme, have marked off Moral Reason from thought and reasoning as they show themselves in ordinary life and in science. They have erected a unique faculty whose sole office is to make us aware of duty and of its imperatively rightful authority over conduct. The moralists who have insisted upon the identity of the Good with ends of desire have, on the contrary, made knowledge, in the sense of insight into the ends which bring enduring satisfaction, the supreme thing in conduct; ignorance, as Plato said, is the root of all evil. And yet, according to Plato, this assured insight into the true End and Good implies a kind of rationality which is radically different from that involved in the ordinary affairs of life. It can be directly attained only by the few who are gifted with those peculiar qualities which enable them to rise to metaphysical understanding of the ultimate constitution of the universe; others must take it on faith or as it is embodied, in a derived way, in laws and institutions. Without going into all the recondite problems associated with the conflict of views, we may say that two significant questions emerge. First, are thought and knowledge mere servants and attendants of emotion, or do they exercise a positive and transforming influence? Secondly, are the thought and judgment employed in connection with moral matters the same that are used in ordinary practical affairs, or are they something separate, having an *exclusively* moral significance? Putting the question in the form which it assumed in discussion during the nineteenth century: Is conscience a faculty of intuition independent of human experience, or is it a product and expression of experience?

The questions are stated in a theoretical form. They have, however, an important practical bearing. They are connected, for example, with the question discussed in the last chapter. Are praise and blame, esteem and condemnation, not only original and spontaneous tendencies, but are they also *ultimate*, incapable of being modified by the critical and constructive work of thought? Again, if conscience is a unique and separate faculty it is incapable of education and modification; it can only be directly appealed to. Most important of all, practically, is that some theories, like the Kantian, make a sharp separation between conduct that is moral and everyday conduct which is morally indifferent and neutral.

It would be difficult to find a question more significant for actual behavior than just this one: Is the moral region isolated from the rest of human activity? Does only one special class of human aims and relations have moral value? This conclusion is a necessary result of the view that our moral consciousness and knowledge is unique in kind. But if moral consciousness is not separate, then no hard and fast line can be drawn within conduct shutting off a moral realm from a non-moral. Now our whole previous discussion is bound up with the latter view. For it has found moral good and excellence in objects

and activities which develop out of natural desires and normal
social relations in family, neighborhood, and community. We
shall accordingly now proceed to make explicit the bearing of
this idea upon the nature of moral insight, comparing our
conclusions with those arrived at by some other typical
theories.

Moral judgments, whatever else they are, are a species of
judgments of *value*. They characterize acts and traits of character as having *worth*, positive or negative. Judgments of
value are not confined to matters which are explicitly moral
in significance. Our estimates of poems, pictures, landscapes,
from the standpoint of their esthetic quality, are value-judgments. Business men are rated with respect to their economic
standing in giving of credit, etc. We do not content ourselves
with a purely external statement about the weather as it is
measured scientifically by the thermometer or barometer.
We term it fine or nasty: epithets of value. Articles of fur-
niture are judged useful, comfortable, or the reverse. Scientifically, the condition of the body and mind can be described in terms which neglect entirely the difference between
health and disease, in terms, that is, of certain physical and
chemical processes. When we pronounce the judgment, "well"
or "ill" we estimate in value terms. When we judge the
statements of others, whether made in casual conversation or
in scientific discourse and pronounce them "true" or "false"
we are making judgments of value. Indeed, the chief embarrassment in giving illustrations of value-judgments is that we
are so constantly engaged in making them. In its popular
sense, *all* judgment is estimation, appraisal, assigning value to
something; a discrimination as to advantage, serviceability,
fitness for a purpose, enjoyability, and so on.

There is a difference which must be noted between valuation
as judgment (which involves thought in placing the thing
judged in its relations and bearings) and valuing as a direct
emotional and practical act. There is difference between

esteem and estimation, between prizing and appraising. To esteem is to prize, hold dear, admire, approve; to estimate is to measure in intellectual fashion. One is direct, spontaneous; the other is reflex, reflective. We esteem before we estimate, and estimation comes in to consider whether and to what extent something is *worthy* of esteem. Is the object one which we *should* admire? Should we really prize it? Does it have the qualities which *justify* our holding it dear? All growth in maturity is attended with this change from a spontaneous to a reflective and critical attitude. First, our affections go out to something in attraction or repulsion; we like and dislike. Then experience raises the question whether the object in question is what our esteem or disesteem took it to be, whether it is such as to justify our reaction to it.

The obvious difference between the two attitudes is that direct admiration and prizing are absorbed in the object, a person, act, natural scene, work of art or whatever, to the neglect of its place and effects, its connections with other things. That a lover does not see the beloved one as others do is notorious, and the principle is of universal application. For to think is to look at a thing in its *relations* with other things, and such judgment often modifies radically the original attitude of esteem and liking. A commonplace instance is the difference between natural liking for some object of food, and the recognition forced upon us by experience that it is not "good" for us, that it is not healthful. A child may like and prize candy inordinately; an adult tells him it is not good for him, that it will make him ill. "Good" to the child signifies that which tastes good; that which satisfies an immediate craving. "Good" from the standpoint of the more experienced person is that which serves certain ends, that which stands in certain connections with consequences. Judgment of value is the name of the act which searches for and takes into consideration these connections.

There is an evident unity between this point and what was said in the last chapter about approval and reprobation, praise and blame. A normal person will not witness an act of wanton cruelty without an immediate response of disfavor; resentment and indignation immediately ensue. A child will respond in this way when some person of whom he is fond is made to suffer by another. An adult, however, may recognize that the one inflicting the suffering is a physician who is doing what he does in the interest of a patient. The child takes the act for what is immediately present to him and finds it bad; the other interprets it as one element in a larger whole and finds it good in that connection. In this change is illustrated in a rudimentary way the processes through which, out of spontaneous acts of favor and disfavor, there develops the idea of a *standard* by which approval and disapproval should be regulated. The change explains the fact that judgments of value are not mere registrations (see p. 110) of previous attitudes of favor and disfavor, liking and aversion, but have a reconstructive and transforming effect upon them, by determining the objects that are worthy of esteem and approbation.

§ 2. THE IMMEDIATE SENSE OF VALUE AND ITS LIMITATIONS

The distinction between direct *valuing*, in the sense of prizing and being absorbed in an object or person, and *valuation* as reflective judgment, based upon consideration of a comprehensive scheme, has an important bearing upon the controversy as to the *intuitive* character of moral judgments. Our immediate responses of approval and reprobation may well be termed intuitive. They are not based upon any thought-out reason or ground. We just admire and resent, are attracted and repelled. This attitude is not only original and primitive but it persists in acquired dispositions. The reaction of an expert in any field is, relatively at least, intuitive rather than reflective. An expert in real estate will, for example, "size up" pecuniary values of land and property with a promptness and exactness which are far beyond the capacity of a layman. A scientifically trained person will see the meaning and possibilities of some line of investigation, where the untrained person might require years of study to make anything out of it. Some persons are happily gifted in their direct appreciation of personal relations; they are noted for tact, not in the sense of a superficial amiability but of real insight into human needs and affections. The results of prior experience, including previous conscious thinking, get taken up into direct habits, and express themselves in direct appraisals of value. Most of our moral judgments are intuitive, but this fact is not a proof of the existence of a separate faculty of moral insight, but is the result of past experience funded into direct outlook upon the scene of life. As Aristotle remarked in effect a long time ago, the immediate judgments of good and evil of a good man are more to be trusted than many of the elaborately reasoned out estimates of the inexperienced.

The immediate character of moral judgments is reënforced by the lessons of childhood and youth. Children are surrounded by adults who constantly pass judgments of value on conduct. And these comments are not coldly intellectual; they are made under conditions of a strongly emotional nature. Pains are taken to stamp them in by impregnating the childish response with elements of awe and mystery, as well as ordinary reward and punishment. The attitudes remain when the circumstances of their origin are forgotten; they are made so much a part of the self that they seem to be inevitable and innate.

This fact, while it explains the intuitive character of reactions, also indicates a limitation of direct valuations. They are often the result of an education which was misdirected. If the conditions of their origin were intelligent, that is, if parents and friends who took part in their creation, were morally wise, they are likely to be intelligent. But arbitrary and irrelevant circumstances often enter in, and leave their impress as surely as do reasonable factors. The very fact of the early origin and now unconscious quality of the attendant intuitions is often distorting and limiting. It is almost impossible for later reflection to get at and correct that which has become unconsciously a part of the self. The warped and distorted will seem natural. Only the conventional and the fanatical are always immediately sure of right and wrong in conduct.

There is a permanent limit to the value of even the best of the intuitive appraisals of which we have been speaking. These are dependable in the degree in which conditions and objects of esteem are fairly uniform and recurrent. They do not work with equal sureness in the cases in which the new and unfamiliar enters in. "New occasions teach new duties." But they cannot teach them to those who suppose that they can trust without further reflection to estimates of the good and evil which are brought over from the past to the new occasion. Extreme intuitionalism and extreme conservatism often go together. Dislike to thoughtful consideration of the requirements of new situations is frequently a sign of fear that the result of examination will be a new insight which will entail the changing of settled habits and will compel departure from easy grooves in behavior—a process which is uncomfortable.

Taken in and of themselves, intuitions or immediate feelings of what is good and bad are of psychological rather than moral import. They are indications of formed habits rather than adequate evidence of what should be approved and disapproved. They afford at most, when habits already existing are of a good character, a *presumption* of correctness, and are guides, clews. But (a) nothing is more immediate and seemingly sure of itself than inveterate prejudice. The morals of a class, clique, or race when brought in contact with those of other races and peoples, are usually so sure of the rectitude of their own judgments of good and bad that they are narrow and give rise to misunderstanding and hostility. (b) A judgment which is adequate under ordinary circumstance may go far astray under changed conditions. It goes without saying that false ideas about values have to be emended; it is not so readily seen that ideas of good and evil which were once true have to be modified as social conditions change. Men become attached to their judgments as they cling to other possessions which familiarity has made dear. Especially in times like the present, when industrial, political, and scientific transformations are rapidly in process, a revision of old appraisals is especially needed. (c) The tendency of undiluted intuitional theory is in the direction of an unquestioning dogmatism, what Bentham called *ipse dixitism*. Every intuition, even the best, is likely to become perfunctory and second-hand unless revitalized by consideration of its meaning —that is, of the consequences which will accrue from acting upon it. There is no necessary connection between a conviction of right and good in general and *what* is right and good in particular. A man may have a strong conviction of duty without enlightenment as to just where his duty lies. When he assumes that because he is actuated by consciousness of duty in general, he can trust without reflective inquiry to his immediate ideas of the particular thing which is his duty, he is likely to become socially dangerous. If he is a person of strong will he will attempt to impose his judgments and standards upon others in a ruthless way, convinced that he is supported by the authority of Right and the Will of God.

§ 3. SENSITIVITY AND THOUGHTFULNESS

The permanent element of value in the intuitional theory lies in its implicit emphasis upon the importance of direct responsiveness to the qualities of situations and acts. A keen eye and a quick ear are not in themselves guarantees of correct knowledge of physical objects. But they are conditions without which such knowledge cannot arise. Nothing can make

up for the absence of immediate sensitiveness; the insensitive
person is callous, indifferent. Unless there is a direct, mainly
unreflective appreciation of persons and deeds, the data for
subsequent thought will be lacking or distorted. A person
must *feel* the qualities of acts as one feels with the hands the
qualities of roughness and smoothness in objects, before he
has an inducement to deliberate or material with which to
deliberate. Effective reflection must also terminate in a
situation which is directly appreciated, if thought is to be
effective in action. "Cold blooded" thought may reach a correct conclusion, but if a person remains anti-pathetic or indifferent to the considerations presented to him in a rational
way, they will not stir him to act in accord with them (see
p. 36).

This fact explains the element of truth in the theories which
insist that in their root and essence moral judgments are
emotional rather than intellectual. A moral judgment, however intellectual it may be, must at least be colored with
feeling if it is to influence behavior. Resentment, ranging
from fierce abhorrence through disgust to mild repugnance,
is a necessary ingredient of knowledge of evil which is genuine
knowledge. Affection, from intense love to mild favor, is an
ingredient in all operative knowledge, all full apprehension,
of the good. It is, however, going too far to say that such
appreciation can dispense with every cognitive element. There
may be no knowledge of *why* a given act calls out sympathy or
antipathy, no knowledge of the grounds upon which it rests
for justification. In fact a strong emotional appreciation
seems at the time to be its own reason and justification. But
there must at least be an idea of the object which is admired or
despised, there must be some perceived cause, or person,
that is cared for, and that solicits concern. Otherwise we
have mere brute anger like the destructive rage of a beast,
or mere immediate gratification like that of an animal in
taking food.

Our sensory reactions, of eye, ear, hand, nose, and tongue supply material of our knowledge of qualities of physical things, sticks, stones, fruits, etc. It is sometimes argued that they afford also the material of our knowledge of persons; that, seeing certain shapes and colors, hearing certain sounds, etc., we infer by analogy that a particular physical body is inhabited by a sentient and emotional being such as we associate with the forms and contacts which compose our own body. The theory is absurd. *Emotional* reactions form the chief materials of our knowledge of ourselves and of others. Just as ideas of physical objects are constituted out of sensory material, so those of persons are framed out of emotional and affectional materials. The latter are as direct, as immediate as the former, and more interesting, with a greater hold on attention. The animism of primitive life, the tendency to personify natural events and things (which survives in poetry), is evidence of the original nature of perception of persons; it is inexplicable on the theory that we infer the existence of persons through a round-about use of analogy. Wherever we strongly hate or love, we tend to predicate directly a lovely and loving, a hateful and hating being. Without emotional behavior, all human beings would be for us only animated automatons. Consequently all actions which call out lively esteem or disfavor are perceived as acts *of* persons: we do not make a distinction in such cases between the doer and the deed. A noble act signifies a noble person; a mean act a mean person.

On this account, the reasonable act and the generous act lie close together. A person entirely lacking in sympathetic response might have a keen calculating intellect, but he would have no spontaneous sense of the claims of others for satisfaction of their desires. A person of narrow sympathy is of necessity a person of confined outlook upon the scene of human good. The only truly *general* thought is the *generous* thought. It is sympathy which carries thought out beyond the self and which extends its scope till it approaches the universal as its limit. It is sympathy which saves consideration of consequences from degenerating into mere calculation, by rendering vivid the interests of others and urging us to give them the same weight as those which touch our own honor, purse, and power. To put ourselves in the place of others, to see things from the standpoint of their purposes and values, to humble, contrariwise, our own pretensions and claims till they reach the level they would assume in the eye of an impartial sympathetic observer, is the surest way to attain objectivity of moral knowledge. Sympathy is the animating mold of moral judgment not because its dictates take precedence in action over those of other impulses (which they do not do), but because it furnishes the most efficacious *intellectual* standpoint. It is the tool, *par excellence*, for resolving complex situations. Then when it passes into active and overt conduct, it does so *fused* with other impulses and not in isolation and is thus protected from sentimentality. In this fusion there is broad and objective survey of all desires and projects because there is an expanded personality. Through sympathy the cold calculation of utilitarianism and the formal law of Kant are transported into vital and moving realities.

One of the earliest discoveries of morals was the similarity of judgment of good and bad in conduct with the recognition of beauty and ugliness in conduct. Feelings of the repulsiveness of vice and the attractiveness of virtuous acts root in esthetic sentiment. Emotions of admiration and of disgust are native; when they are turned upon conduct they form an element which furnishes the truth that lies in the theory of a moral *sense*. The sense of justice, moreover, has a strong ally in the sense of symmetry and proportion. The double meaning of the term "fair" is no accident. The Greek *sophrosyne* (of which our temperance, through the Latin *temperentia*, is a poor representation), a harmonious blending of affections into a beautiful whole, was essentially an artistic idea. Self-control was its inevitable *result*, but self-control as a deliberate cause would have seemed as abhorrent to the Athenian as would "control" in a building or statue where control signified anything other than the idea of the whole permeating all parts and bringing them into order and measured unity. The Greek emphasis upon *Kalokagathos*, the Aristotleian identification of virtue with the proportionate mean, are indications of an acute estimate of grace, rhythm, and harmony as dominant traits of good conduct. The modern mind has been much less sensitive to esthetic values in general and to these values in conduct in particular. Much has been lost in direct responsiveness to right. The bleakness and harshness often associated with morals is a sign of this loss.

The direct valuing which accompanies immediate sensitive responsiveness to acts has its complement and expansion in valuations which are deliberate, reflective. As Aristotle pointed out, only the good man is a good judge of what is truly good; it takes a fine and well-grounded character to react immediately with the right approvals and condemnations. And to this statement must be added two qualifications. One is that even the good man can trust for enlightenment to his direct responses of values only in simpler situations, in those which are already upon the whole familiar. The better he is, the more likely he is to be perplexed as to what to do in novel, complicated situations. Then the only way out is through examination, inquiry, turning things over in his mind till something presents itself, perhaps after prolonged mental fermentation, to which he can directly react. The other qualification is that there is no such thing as a good man—in an absolute sense. Immediate appreciation is liable to be warped by many considerations which can be detected and uprooted only through inquiry and criticism. To be completely good and an infallible judge of right a man would have had to live from infancy in a thoroughly good social medium free from all limiting and distorting influences. As it is, habits of liking and disliking are formed early in life, prior to ability to use discriminating intelligence. Prejudices, unconscious biases, are generated; one is uneven in his distribution of esteem and admiration; he is unduly sensitive to some values, relatively indifferent to others. He is set in his ways, and his immediate appreciations travel in the grooves laid down by his unconsciously formed habits. Hence the spontaneous "intuitions" of value have to be entertained subject to correction, to confirmation and revision, by personal observation of consequences and cross-questioning of their quality and scope.

§ 4. CONSCIENCE AND DELIBERATION

The usual name for this process is deliberation; the name given moral deliberativeness when it is habitual is conscientiousness. This quality is constituted by scrupulous attentiveness to the potentialities of any act or proposed aim. Its possession is a characteristic of those who do not allow themselves to be unduly swayed by immediate appetite and passion, nor to fall into ruts of routine behavior. The "good" man who rests on his oars, who permits himself to be propelled simply by the momentum of his attained right habits, loses alertness; he ceases to be on the lookout. With that loss, his goodness drops away from him. There is, indeed, a quality called "overconscientiousness," but it is not far from a vice. It signifies constant anxiety as to whether one is really good or not, a moral "self-consciousness" which spells embarrassment, constraint in action, morbid fear. It is a caricature of genuine conscientiousness. For the latter is not an anxious prying into motives, a fingering of the inner springs of action to detect whether or not a "motive" is good. Genuine conscientiousness has an objective outlook; it is intelligent attention and care to the quality of an act in view of its consequences for general happiness; it is not anxious solicitude for one's own virtuous state.

Perhaps the most striking difference between immediate sensitiveness, or "intuition," and "conscientiousness" as reflective interest, is that the former tends to rest upon the plane of achieved goods, while the latter is on the outlook for something *better*. The truly conscientious person not only uses a standard in judging, but is concerned to revise and improve his standard. He realizes that the value resident in acts goes beyond anything which he has already apprehended, and that therefore there must be something inadequate in any standard which has been definitely formulated. He is on the *lookout* for good not already achieved. Only by thoughtfulness does one become sensitive to the far-reaching implications of an act; apart from continual reflection we are at best sensitive only to the value of special and limited ends.

The larger and remoter values of an act form what is ordinarily termed an ideal. About nothing, perhaps, is misconception more current than as to the nature of ideals. They are thought of sometimes as fixed, remote goals, too far away to be ever realized in conduct and sometimes as vague emotional inspirations which take the place of thought in directing conduct. Thus the "idealist" is thought of as either an impractical person, concerned with the unattainable, or else as a person who is moved by aspirations for something intangible of a vague spiritual sort having no concrete reference to actual situations. The trouble with ideals of remote "perfection" is that they tend to make us negligent of the significance of the special situations in which we have to act; they are thought of as trivial in comparison with the ideal of perfection. The genuine ideal, on the contrary, is the sense that each of these special situations brings with it its own inexhaustible meaning, that its value reaches far beyond its direct local existence. Its nature is perhaps best expressed in the verses of George Herbert:

> Who sweeps a room as for Thy Laws
> Makes that and th' action fine.

As we have said, reflection when directed to practical matters, to determination of what to do, is called deliberation. A general deliberates upon the conduct of a campaign, weighing possible moves of the enemy and of his own troops, considering pros and cons; a business man deliberates in comparing various modes of investment; a lawyer deliberates upon the conduct of his case, and so on. In all cases of deliberation, judgment of *value* enters; the one who engages in it is concerned to weigh values with a view to discovering the better and rejecting the worse. In some cases, the value of ends is thought of and in other cases the value of means. Moral deliberation differs from other forms not as a process of forming a judgment and arriving at knowledge but in the kind of value which is thought about. The value is technical, professional, economic, etc., as long as one thinks of it as something which one can aim at and attain by way of having, *possessing;* as something to be got or to be missed. Precisely the same object will have a moral value when it is thought of as making a difference in the *self*, as determining what one will *be*, instead of merely what one will *have*. Deliberation involves doubt, hesitation, the need of making up one's mind, of arriving at a decisive choice. The choice at stake in a moral deliberation or valuation is the worth of this and that kind of character and disposition. Deliberation is not then to be identified with calculation, or a quasi-mathematical reckoning of profit and loss. Such calculation assumes that the nature of the self does not enter into question, but only how much the self is going to *get* of this and that. Moral deliberation deals not with quantity of value but with quality.

We estimate the import or significance of any present desire or impulse by forecasting what it will come or amount to if carried out; literally its consequences define its *consequence*, its meaning or import. But if these consequences are conceived *merely as remote*, if their picturing does not arouse a present sense of peace, of fulfillment, or of dissatisfaction, of incompletion and irritation, the process of thinking out consequences remains purely intellectual. It is as barren of influence upon behavior as the mathematical speculations of a disembodied angel. Any actual experience of reflection upon conduct will show that every foreseen result at once stirs our present affections, our likes and dislikes, our desires and aversions. There is developed a running commentary which stamps objects at once as good or evil. It is this direct sense of value, not the consciousness of general rules or ultimate goals, which finally determines the worth of the act to the agent. Here is an inexpugnable element of truth in the intuitional theory. Its error lies in conceiving this immediate response of appreciation as if it excluded reflection instead of following directly upon its heels. Deliberation is actually an imaginative rehearsal of various courses of conduct. We give way, *in our mind*, to some impulse; we try, *in our mind*, some plan. Following its career through various steps, we find ourselves in imagination in the presence of the consequences that would follow: and as we then like and approve, or dislike and disapprove, these consequences, we find the original impulse or plan good or bad. Deliberation is dramatic and active, not mathematical and impersonal; and hence it has the intuitive, the direct factor in it. The advantage of a mental trial, prior to the overt trial (for the act after all is itself also a trial, a proving of the idea that lies back of it), is that it is retrievable, whereas overt consequences remain. They cannot be recalled. Moreover, many trials may mentally be made in a short time. The imagining of various plans carried out furnishes an opportunity for many impulses which at first are not in evidence at all, to get under way. Many and varied direct sensings, appreciations, take place. When many tendencies are brought into play, there is clearly much greater probability that the capacity of self which is really needed and appropriate will be brought into action, and thus a truly reasonable happiness result. The tendency of deliberation to "polarize" the various lines of activity into opposed alternatives, into incompatible "either this or that," is a way of forcing into clear recognition the importance of the issue.

§ 5. THE NATURE AND OFFICE OF PRINCIPLES

It is clear that the various situations in which a person is called to deliberate and judge have common elements, and that values found in them resemble one another. It is also obvious that general ideas are a great aid in judging particular cases. If different situations were wholly unlike one another, nothing could be learned from one which would be of any avail in any other. But having like points, experience carries over from one to another, and experience is intellectually cumulative. Out of resembling experiences general ideas develop; through language, instruction, and tradition this gathering together of experiences of value into generalized points of view is extended to take in a whole people and a race. Through intercommunication the experience of the entire human race is to some extent pooled and crystallized in general ideas. These ideas constitute *principles*. We bring them with us to deliberation on particular situations.

These generalized points of view are of great use in surveying particular cases. But as they are transmitted from one generation to another, they tend to become fixed and rigid. Their origin in experience is forgotten and so is their proper use in further experience. They are thought of as if they existed in and of themselves and as if it were simply a question of bringing action under them in order to determine what is right and good. Instead of being treated as aids and instruments in judging values as the latter actually arise, they are made superior to them. They become prescriptions, rules. Now a genuine principle differs from a rule in two ways: (a) A principle evolves in connection with the course of experience, being a generalized statement of what sort of consequences and values tend to be realized in certain kinds of situations;

a rule is taken as something ready-made and fixed. (b) A principle is primarily intellectual, a method and scheme for judging, and is practical secondarily because of what it discloses; a rule is primarily practical.

Suppose that one is convinced that the rule of honesty is made known just in and of itself by a special faculty, and has absolutely nothing to do with recollection of past cases or forecast of possible future circumstances. How would such a rule apply itself to any particular case which needed to be judged? What bell would ring, what signal would be given, to indicate that just *this* case is the appropriate case for the application of the rule of honest dealing? And if by some miracle this question were answered, if we could know that here is a case for the rule of honesty, how should we know just what course in detail the rule calls for? For the rule, to be applicable to all cases, must omit the conditions which differentiate one case from another; it must contain only the very few similar elements which are to be found in all honest deeds. Reduced to this skeleton, not much would be left save the bare injunction to be honest whatever happens, leaving it to chance, the ordinary judgment of the individual, or to external authority to find out just *what* honesty specifically means in the given case.

This difficulty is so serious that all systems which have committed themselves to belief in a number of hard and fast rules having their origin in conscience, or in the word of God impressed upon the human soul or externally revealed, always have had to resort to a more and more complicated procedure to cover, if possible, all the cases. The moral life is finally reduced by them to an elaborate formalism and legalism.

Suppose, for example, we take the Ten Commandments as a starting-point. They are only ten, and naturally confine themselves to general ideas, and ideas stated mainly in negative form. Moreover, the same act may be brought under

more than one rule. In order to resolve the practical perplex-
ities and uncertainties which inevitably arise under such circumstances, *Casuistry* is built up (from the Latin *casus*, case).
The attempt is made to foresee all the different cases of action
which may conceivably occur, and provide in advance the
exact rule for each case. For example, with reference to the
rule "do not kill," a list will be made of all the different situations in which killing might occur:—accident, war, fulfillment
of command of political superior (as by a hangman), self-
defense (defense of one's own life, of others, of property),
deliberate or premeditated killing with its different motives
(jealousy, avarice, revenge, etc.), killing with slight premedita-
tion, from sudden impulse, from different sorts and degrees
of provocation. To each one of these possible cases is assigned
its exact moral quality, its exact degree of turpitude and inno-
cency. Nor can this process end with overt acts; all the inner
springs of action which affect regard for life must be similarly
classified: envy, animosity, sudden rage, sullenness, cherishing
of sense of injury, love of tyrannical power, hardness or hostility, callousness—all these must be specified into their different
kinds and the exact moral worth of each determined. What is
done for this one kind of case must be done for every part
and phase of the entire moral life until it is all inventoried,
catalogued, and distributed into pigeon-holes definitely labeled.

Dangers and evils attend this way of conceiving the moral
life. (a) *It tends to magnify the letter of morality at the expense
of its spirit.* It fixes attention not upon the positive good in an
act, not upon the underlying agent's disposition which forms its
spirit, nor upon the unique occasion and context which form
its atmosphere, but upon its literal conformity with Rule A,
Class I., Species 1, subhead (1), etc. The effect of this is
inevitably to narrow the scope and lessen the depth of conduct. (i.) It tempts some to hunt for that classification of
their act which will make it the most convenient or profitable
for themselves. In popular speech, "casuistical" has come to

mean a way of judging acts which splits hairs in the effort to find a way of acting that conduces to personal interest and profit, and which yet may be justified by some moral principle. (ii.) With others, this regard for the letter makes conduct formal and pedantic. It gives rise to a rigid and hard type of character conventionally attributed to the Pharisees of olden and the Puritans of modern time—the moral schemes of both classes being strongly impregnated with the notion of fixed moral rules.

(b) *This ethical system also tends in practice to a legal view of conduct.* Historically it always has sprung from carrying over legal ideas into morality. In the legal view liability to blame and to punishment inflicted from without by some superior authority, is necessarily prominent. Conduct is regulated through specific injunctions and prohibitions: Do this, Do not do that. Exactly the sort of analysis of which we have spoken above (p. 306) in the case of killing is necessary, so that there may be definite and regular methods of measuring guilt and assigning blame. Now liability, punishment, and reward are important factors in the conduct of life, but any scheme of morals is defective which puts the question of avoiding punishment in the foreground of attention, or which tends to create a pharisaical complacency in the mere fact of having conformed to command or rule.

(c) *Probably the worst evil of this moral system is that it tends to deprive moral life of freedom and spontaneity* and to reduce it (especially for the conscientious who take it seriously) to a more or less anxious and servile conformity to externally imposed rules. Obedience as loyalty to principle is a good, but this scheme practically makes it the only good and conceives it not as loyalty to ideals, but as conformity to commands. Moral rules exist just as independent deliverances on their own account, and the right thing is merely to follow them. This puts the center of moral gravity outside the concrete processes of living. All systems which emphasize the letter more than

the spirit, legal consequences more than vital motives, put
the individual under the weight of external authority. They
lead to the kind of conduct described by St. Paul as under
the law, not in the spirit, with its constant attendant weight
of anxiety, uncertain struggle, and impending doom.

Many who strenuously object to all of these schemes of
conduct, to everything which hardens it into forms by em-
phasizing external commands, authority, and punishments and
rewards, fail to see that such evils are logically connected
with any acceptance of the finality of fixed rules. They hold
certain bodies of people, religious officers, political or legal
authorities, responsible for what they object to in the scheme;
while they still cling to the idea that morality is an effort to
apply to particular deeds and projects a certain number of
absolute unchanging moral rules. They fail to see that, if
this were its nature, those who attempt to provide the machinery which would render it practically workable deserve
praise rather than blame. In fact, the notion of absolute rules
or precepts cannot be made workable except through certain
superior authorities who declare and enforce them.   Said
Locke: "It is no small power it gives one man over another
to be the dictator of principles and teacher of unquestionable
truths."

There is another practically harmful consequence which
follows from the identification of principles with rules. Take
the case of, say, justice. There may be all but universal
agreement in the notion that justice is the proper rule of
conduct—so universal as to be admitted by all but criminals.
But just what does justice demand in the concrete? The
present state of such things as penology, prison reform, the
tariff, sumptuary laws, trusts, the relation of capital and labor,
collective bargaining, democratic government, private or public ownership of public utilities, communal versus private
property, shows that persons of equally well-meaning dispositions find that justice means opposite things in practice,

although all proclaim themselves devoted to justice as the rule of action. Taken as a principle, not as a rule, justice signifies the will to *examine* specific institutions and measures so as to find out how they operate with the view of introducing greater impartiality and equity into the consequences they produce.

This consideration brings us to the important fact regarding the nature of true moral principles. *Rules are practical; they are habitual ways of doing things. But principles are intellectual; they are the final methods used in judging suggested courses of action.* The fundamental error of the intuitionalist is that he is on the outlook for rules which will of themselves tell agents just what course of action to pursue; *whereas the object of moral principles is to supply standpoints and methods which will enable the individual to make for himself an analysis of the elements of good and evil in the particular situation in which he finds himself.* No genuine moral principle prescribes a specific course of action; rules,[1] like cooking recipes, may tell just what to do and how to do it. A moral principle, such as that of chastity, of justice, of the Golden Rule, gives the agent a basis for looking at and examining a particular question that comes up. It holds before him certain possible aspects of the act; it warns him against taking a short or partial view of the act. It economizes his thinking by supplying him with the main heads by reference to which to consider the bearings of his desires and purposes; it guides him in his thinking by suggesting to him the important considerations for which he should be on the lookout.

A moral principle, then, is not a command to act or forbear acting in a given way: *it is a tool for analyzing a special situation*, the right or wrong being determined by the situation in its entirety, and not by the rule as such. We sometimes hear it

---

[1] Of course, the word "rule" is often used to designate a principle—as in the case of the phrase "Golden Rule." We are speaking not of the words, but of their underlying ideas.

stated, for example, that the universal adoption of the Golden Rule would at once settle all industrial disputes and difficulties. But suppose that the principle were accepted in good faith by everybody; it would not at once tell everybody just what to do in all the complexities of his relations to others. When individuals are still uncertain of what their real good may be, it does not finally decide matters to tell them to regard the good of others as they would their own. Nor does it mean that whatever in detail we want for ourselves we should strive to give to others. Because I am fond of classical music it does not follow that I should thrust as much of it as possible upon my neighbors. But the "Golden Rule" does furnish us a *point of view from which to consider acts;* it suggests the necessity of considering how our acts affect the interests of others as well as our own; it tends to prevent partiality of regard; it warns against setting an undue estimate upon a particular conse- quence of pain or pleasure, simply because it happens to affect us. In short, the Golden Rule does not issue special orders or commands; but it does clarify and illuminate the situations requiring intelligent deliberation.

The same distinction is implied in what was brought out in the last chapter between happiness (in the sense of general welfare) as an end and as a standard. If it were regarded as the direct end of acts, it might be taken to be something fixed and inflexible. As a standard it is rather a cautionary direction, saying that when we judge an act, accomplished or proposed, with reference to approval and disapproval, we should first consider its consequences in general, and then its special consequences with respect to whatever affects the well-being of others. As a standard it provides a consistent point of view to be taken in all deliberation, but it does not pretend to determine in advance precisely what constitutes the general welfare or common good. It leaves room open for discovery of new constituents of well-being, and for varying combinations of these constituents in different situations. If the standard were taken as a rule, in the sense of a recipe, it would signify that one comes to each case with a prior hard and fast, Procrustean, and complete conception of just and only what elements form happiness, so that this conception can be applied like a mathematical formula. "Standards" interpreted after this fashion breed self-righteousness, moral conceit, and fanaticism. The standard as a standpoint for survey of situations allows free play to the imagination in reaching new insights. It requires, rather than merely permits, continual advance in the conception of what constitutes happiness in the concrete.

It follows accordingly that the important thing about knowledge in its moral aspect is not its actual extent so much as it is the *will* to know—the active desire to examine conduct in its bearing upon the general good. Actual information and insight are limited by conditions of birth, education, social environment. The notion of the intuitional theory that all persons possess a uniform and equal stock of moral judgments is contrary to fact. Yet there are common human affections and impulses which express themselves within every social environment;—there is no people the members of which do not have a belief in the value of human life, of care of offspring, of loyalty to tribal and community customs, etc., however restricted and one-sided they may be in the application of these beliefs. Beyond this point, there is always, on whatever level of culture, the possibility of being on the alert for opportunities to widen and deepen the meaning of existing moral ideas. The attitude of *seeking* for what is good may be cultivated under any conditions of race, class, and state of civilization. Persons who are ignorant in the conventional sense of education may display an interest in discovering and considering what is good which is absent in the highly literate and polished. From the standpoint of this interest, class divisions vanish. The moral quality of knowledge lies not in possession but in concern with increase. The essential evil of

fixed standards and rules is that it tends to render men
satisfied with the existing state of affairs and to take the
ideas and judgments they already possess as adequate and
final.

The need for constant revision and expansion of moral
knowledge is one great reason why there is no gulf dividing
non-moral knowledge from that which is truly moral. At
any moment conceptions which once seemed to belong exclusively to the biological or physical realm may assume
moral import. This will happen whenever they are discovered
to have a bearing on the common good. When knowledge of
bacteria and germs and their relation to the spread of disease
was achieved, sanitation, public and private, took on a moral
significance it did not have before. For they were seen to
affect the health and well-being of the community. Psychi-
atrists and psychologists working within their own technical
regions have brought to light facts and principles which profoundly affect old conceptions of, say, punishment and responsibility, especially in their place in the formation of disposition. It has been discovered, for example, that "problem
children" are created by conditions which exist in families
and in the reaction of parents to the young. In a rough way,
it may be asserted that most of the morbid conditions of mind
and character which develop later have their origin in emotional arrests and maladjustments of early life. These facts
have not as yet made their way very far into popular understanding and action, but their ultimate moral import is in-
calculable. Knowledge once technically confined to physics
and chemistry is applied in industry and has an effect on the
lives and happiness of individuals beyond all estimate. The
list of examples might be extended indefinitely. The important
point is that any restriction of moral knowledge and judgments
to a definite realm necessarily limits our perception of moral
significance. A large part of the difference between those
who are stagnant and reactionary and those who are gen-

uinely progressive in social matters comes from the fact
that the former think of morals as confined, boxed, within a
round of duties and sphere of values which are fixed and final.
Most of the serious moral problems of the present time are
dependent for their solution upon a general realization that
the contrary is the case. Probably the great need of the present
time is that the traditional barriers between scientific and
moral knowledge be broken down, so that there will be organized and consecutive endeavor to use all available scientific
knowledge for humane and social ends.

There is, therefore, little need of calling attention to the
point with which we have concluded the previous chapters:
namely, the influence of the social environment upon the
chief ethical concepts. Only if some rigid form of intuitionalism
were true, would the state of culture and the growth of knowledge in forms usually called non-moral, be without significance
for distinctively moral knowledge and judgment. Because
the two things are connected, each generation, especially one
living in a time like the present, is under the responsibility
of overhauling its inherited stock of moral principles and
reconsidering them in relation to contemporary conditions
and needs. It is stupid to suppose that this signifies that all
moral principles are so relative to a particular state of society
that they have no binding force in any social condition. The
obligation is to discover *what* principles *are* relevant to our
own social estate. Since this social condition is a fact, the
principles which are related to it are real and significant,
even though they be not adapted to some other set and style
of social institutions, culture, and scientific knowledge. It is
the insistence on a uniform and unchanging code of morals,
the same at all times and places, which brings about the extreme revolt which says that they are all conventional and of
no validity. Recognition of their close and vital relationship
to social forces will create and reënforce search for the principles which are truly relevant in our own day.

LITERATURE

Original material for the earlier history of intuitionalism is found in Selby-Bigge, *British Moralists*, I. and II., from Butler and Price respectively. Selections from Butler, Price, and Reid are found in Rand's *Classical Moralists*. For the "moral sense" theory, see Shaftesbury, *Characteristics;* Hutcheson, *System of Moral Philosophy*. Consult also Sidgwick, *History of Ethics, passim;* and Rogers, *Morals in Review*, 1927. Bonar, *Moral Sense*, 1930, contains an excellent account of the development of the moral sense theory in British thought.

For the relation between sympathy and moral judgment, see Smith, *Theory of Moral Sentiments*, especially Part III., chs. i. and iv., and Part IV., chs. i.–iii., and Stephen, *Science of Ethics*, 1882, pp. 228–238.

For the controversy between the emotional and rational theories of moral judgment see Rashdall, *Is Conscience an Emotion?* 1914, defending the rational theory against McDougall, *Social Psychology*, 1909, and Westermarck, *The Origin and Development of Moral Ideas*, 1906. Fite's *Moral Philosophy*, 1925, is noteworthy for the importance attached to insight in the moral life. See also Aristotle, *Ethics*, Book III., chs. ii.–iii., and Book VI. The nature of deliberation is discussed at greater length in Dewey, *Human Nature and Conduct*, 1922, pp. 189–209. Dewey, *The Quest for Certainty*, 1930, ch. viii., discusses the difference between the immediate sense of value and the judgment of value.

For intuitionalism, see Calderwood, *Handbook of Moral Philosophy;* Maurice, *Conscience;* Whewell, *The Elements of Morality;* Martineau, *Types of Ethical Theory*, Vol. II., 1901, pp. 96–115; Mezes, *Ethics*, 1901, ch. iii.; Sidgwick, *Methods of Ethics*, Book I., chs. viii.–ix., and Book III. entire, but especially ch. i.; *History of Ethics,* pp. 170–204, and 224–236, and *Lectures on Ethics of Green, Spencer, and Martineau*, 1902, pp. 361–374.

CHAPTER VI

THE MORAL SELF

§ 1. THE SELF AND CHOICE

THE self has occupied a central place in the previous discussions, in which important aspects of the good self have been brought out. The self should be *wise* or prudent, looking to an inclusive satisfaction and hence subordinating the satisfaction of an immediately urgent single appetite; it should be *faithful* in acknowledgment of the claims involved in its relations with others; it should be solicitous, *thoughtful*, in the award of praise and blame, use of approbation and disapprobation, and, finally, should be *conscientious* and have the active will to discover new values and to revise former notions. We have not, however, examined just what is the significance of the self. The important position of the self in morals, and also various controversies of moral theory which have gathered about it, make such an examination advisable. A brief reference to the opposed theories will help to indicate the points which need special attention.

A most profound line of cleavage has appeared in topics already discussed. Some theories hold that the self, apart from what it does, is the supreme and exclusive moral end. This view is contained in Kant's assertion that the Good Will, aside from consequences of acts performed, is the only Moral Good. A similar idea is implicit whenever moral goodness is identified in an exclusive way with virtue, so that the final aim of a good person is, when summed up briefly, to maintain his own virtue. When the self is assumed to be the *end* in an exclusive way, then conduct, acts, consequences, are all treated as *mere* means, as external instruments for maintaining the

147

good self. The opposed point of view is found in the hedonism of the earlier utilitarians when they assert that a certain kind of consequences, pleasure, is the only good end and that the self and its qualities are mere means for producing these consequences.

Our own theory gives both self and consequences indispensable rôles. We have held, by implication, that neither one can be made to be merely a means to the other. There is a circular arrangement. The self is not a *mere* means to producing consequences because the consequences, when of a moral kind, enter into the formation of the self and the self enters into them. To use a somewhat mechanical analogy, bricks are means to building a house, but they are not *mere* means because they finally *compose* a part of the house itself; if being a part of the house then reacted to modify the nature of the bricks themselves the analogy would be quite adequate. Similarly, conduct and consequences are important, but instead of being separate from the self they form, reveal, and test the self. That which has just been stated in a formal way will be given concrete meaning if we consider the nature of choice, since choice is the most characteristic activity of a self.

Prior to anything which may be called choice in the sense of deliberate decision come spontaneous selections or *preferences*. Every appetite and impulse, however blind, is a mode of preferring one thing to another; it selects one thing and re jects others. It goes out with attraction to certain objects, putting them ahead of others in value. The latter are neglected although from a purely external standpoint they are equally accessible and available. We are so constructed that both by original temperament and by acquired habit we move toward some objects rather than others. Such preference antecedes judgment of comparative values; it is organic rather than conscious. Afterwards there arise situations in which wants compete; we are drawn spontaneously in opposite directions.

Incompatible preferences hold each other in check. We hesitate, and then hesitation becomes deliberation: that weighing of values in comparison with each other of which we have already spoken. At last, a preference emerges which is intentional and which is based on consciousness of the values which deliberation has brought into view. We have to make up our minds, when we want two conflicting things, which of them we *really* want. That is choice. We prefer spontaneously, we choose deliberately, knowingly.

Now every such choice sustains a double relation to the self. It reveals the existing self and it forms the future self. That which is chosen is that which is found congenial to the desires and habits of the self as it already exists. Deliberation has an important function in this process, because each different possibility as it is presented to the imagination appeals to a different element in the constitution of the self, thus giving all sides of character a chance to play their part in the final choice. The resulting choice also shapes the self, making it, in some degree, a new self. This fact is especially marked at critical junctures (p. 14), but it marks every choice to some extent however slight. Not all are as momentous as the choice of a calling in life, or of a life-partner. But every choice is at the forking of the roads, and the path chosen shuts off certain opportunities and opens others. In committing oneself to a particular course, a person gives a lasting set to his own being. Consequently, it is proper to say that in choosing this object rather than that, one is in reality choosing what kind of person or self one is going to be. Superficially, the deliberation which terminates in choice is concerned with weighing the values of particular ends. Below the surface, it is a process of discovering what sort of being a person most wants to become.

Selfhood or character is thus not a *mere* means, an external instrument, of attaining certain ends. It *is* an agency of accomplishing consequences, as is shown in the pains which the athlete, the lawyer, the merchant, takes to build up certain habits in himself, because he knows they are the causal conditions for reaching the ends in which he is interested. But the self is more than an external causal agent. The attainment of consequences reacts to form the self. Moreover, as Aristotle said, the goodness of a good man shines through his deeds. We say of one another's conduct, "How characteristic that was!" In using such an expression we imply that the self is more than a cause of an act in the sense in which a match is a cause of a fire; we imply that the self has entered so intimately into the act performed as to qualify it. The self reveals its nature in what it chooses. In consequence a moral judgment upon an act is also a judgment upon the character or selfhood of the one doing the act. Every time we hold a person responsible for what he has done, we acknowledge in effect that a deed which can be judged morally has an intimate and internal connection with the character of the one from whom the deed issued. Metaphorically, we speak of the virtues of a medicinal plant, meaning that it is efficient for producing certain effects which are wanted, but the virtuous dispositions of the self enter into what the self does and remain there, giving the act its special quality.

If the earlier utilitarians erred in thinking that the self with its virtuous and vicious dispositions was of importance only as a means to certain consequences in which all genuine good and evil are found, the school which holds that consequences have no moral significance at all, and that only the self is morally good and bad, also falls into the error of separating the self and its acts. For goodness and badness could, on this theory, be attributed to the self apart from the results of its dispositions when the latter are put into operation. In truth, only that self is good which wants and strives energetically for good consequences; that is, those consequences which promote the well-being of those affected by the act. It is not too much to say that the key to a correct theory of morality is recognition of the *essential unity of the self and its acts*, if the latter have any moral significance; while errors in theory arise as soon as the self and acts (and their consequences) are separated from each other, and moral worth is attributed to one more than to the other.

The unity of self and action underlies all judgment that is distinctively moral in character. We may judge a happening to be useful or harmful in its consequences, as when we speak of a kindly rain or a destructive torrent. We do not, however, imply moral valuation, because we do not impute connection with character or with a self to rain or flood. On similar grounds, we do not attribute moral quality to acts of an infant, an imbecile or a madman. Yet there comes a time in the life of a normal child when his acts are morally judged. Nevertheless, this fact does not imply, necessarily, that he deliberately intended to produce just the consequences which occurred. It is enough if the judgment is a factor in *forming* a self from which future acts deliberately, intentionally, proceed. A child snatches at food because he is hungry. He is told that he is rude or greedy—a moral judgment. Yet the only thing in the child's mind may have been that the food taken would satisfy hunger. To him the act had no moral import. In calling him rude and greedy, the parent has made a connection between something in himself and a certain quality in his act. The act was performed in a way which discloses something undesirable in the self. If the act be passed without notice, that tendency will be strengthened; the self will be shaped in that direction. On the other hand, if the child can be brought to see the connection, the intimate unity, of his own being and the obnoxious quality of the act, his self will take on another form.

§ 2. THE SELF AND MOTIVATION: INTERESTS

The identity of self and an act, morally speaking, is the key to understanding the nature of *motives* and *motivation*. Unless this unity is perceived and acknowledged in theory, a motive will be regarded as something external acting upon an individual and inducing him to do something. When this point of view is generalized, it leads to the conclusion that the self is naturally, intrinsically, inert and passive, and so has to be stirred or moved to action by something outside itself. The fact, however, is that the self, like its vital basis the organism, is always active; that it acts by its very constitution, and hence needs no external promise of reward or threat of evil to induce it to act. This fact is a confirmation of the moral unity of self and action.

Observation of a child, even a young baby, will convince the observer that a normal human being when awake is engaged in activity; he is a reservoir of energy that is continually overflowing. The organism moves, reaches, handles, pulls, pounds, tears, molds, crumples, looks, listens, etc. It is continually, while awake, exploring its surroundings and establishing new contacts and relations. Periods of quiescence and rest are of course needed for recuperation. But nothing is more intolerable to a healthy human being than enforced passivity over a long period. It is not action that needs to be accounted for, but rather the cessation of activity.

As was intimated earlier in another context, this fact is fatal to a hedonistic psychology (p. 41). Since we act before we have experience of pleasures and pains, since the latter follow as results of action, it cannot possibly be true that desire for pleasure is the source of conduct. The implications of the fact extend, moreover, to the entire concept of motivation. The theory that a motive is an inducement which operates from without upon the self confuses motive and *stimulus*. Stimuli from the environment are highly important factors in conduct. But they are not important as causes, as generators of action. For the organism is already active, and stimuli themselves arise and are experienced only in the course of action. The painful heat of an object stimulates the hand to withdraw but the heat was experienced in the course of reaching and exploring. The function of a stimulus is—as the case just cited illustrates—to *change the direction of an action* already going on. Similarly, a response to a stimulus is not the beginning of activity; it is a *change*, a shift, of activity in response to the change in conditions indicated by a stimulus. A navigator of a ship perceives a headland; this may operate to make him alter the course which his ship takes. But it is not the cause or "moving spring" of his sailing. Motives, like stimuli, induce us to alter the trend and course of our conduct, but they do not evoke or originate action as such.

The term "motive" is thus ambiguous. It means (1) those *interests* which form the core of the self and supply the principles by which conduct is to be understood. It also (2) signifies the *object*, whether perceived or thought of, which effect an alteration in the direction of activity. Unless we bear in mind the connection between these two meanings along with the fundamental character of the first signification, we shall have a wrong conception of the relation of the self to conduct, and this original error will generate error in all parts of ethical theory.

Any concrete case of the union of the self in action with an object and end is called an interest. Children form the interest of a parent; painting or music is the interest of an artist; the concern of a judge is the equable settling of legal disputes; healing of the sick is the interest of a physician. An interest is, in short, the dominant direction of activity, and in this activity desire is united with an object to be furthered in a decisive choice. Unless impulse and desire are enlisted, one has no heart for a course of conduct; one is indifferent, averse, not-interested. On the other hand, an interest is objective; the heart is set on something. There is no interest at large or in a vacuum; each interest imperatively demands an object to which it is attached and for the well-being or development of which it is actively solicitous. If a man says he is interested in pictures, he asserts that he *cares* for them; if he does not go near them, if he takes no pains to create opportunities for viewing and studying them, his actions so belie his words that we know his interest is merely nominal. Interest *is* regard, concern, solicitude, for an object; if it is not manifested in action it is unreal.

A motive is not then a drive *to* action, or something which moves *to* doing something. It *is* the movement of the self as a whole, a movement in which desire is integrated with an object so completely as to be chosen as a compelling end. The hungry person seeks food. We may say, if we please, that he is moved by hunger. But in fact hunger is only a name for the tendency to move toward the appropriation of food. To create an entity out of this active relation of the self to objects, and then to treat this abstraction as if it were the cause of seeking food is sheer confusion. The case is no different when we say that a man is moved by kindness, or mercy, or cruelty, or malice. These things are not independent powers which stir to action. They are designations of the kind of active union or integration which exists between the self and a class of objects. It is the man himself in his very self who is malicious or kindly, and these adjectives signify that the self is so constituted as to act in certain ways towards certain objects. Benevolence or cruelty is not something which a man *has*, as he may have dollars in his pocket-book; it is something which he *is;* and since his being is active, these qualities are *modes of activity*, not forces which produce action.

Because an interest or motive is the union in action of a need, desire of a self, with a chosen object, the object itself may, in a secondary and derived sense, be said to be the motive of action. Thus a bribe may be called the motive which induces a legislator to vote for a particular measure, or profit-making may be called the motive a grocer has for giving just weights. It is clear, however, that it is the person's own make-up which gives the bribe, or the hoped for gain, its hold over him. The avaricious man is stirred to action by objects which mean nothing to a generous person; a frank and open character is moved by objects which would only repel a person of a sly and crafty disposition. A legislator is tempted by a bribe to vote against conviction only because his selfhood is already such that money gain has more value to him than convictions and principles. It is true enough when we take the whole situation into account that an object moves a person; for that object as a moving force *includes the self within it.* Error arises when we think of the object as if it were something wholly external to the make-up of the self, which then operates to move the foreign self.

The secondary and derived sense that identifies "motive" with the object which brings about an *alteration* in the course of conduct has a definite and important practical meaning. In a world like ours where people are associated together, and where what one person does has important consequences for other persons, attempt to influence the action of other persons so that they will do certain things and not do other things is a constant function of life. On all sorts of grounds, we are constantly engaged in trying to influence the conduct of others. Such influencing is the most conspicuous phase of education in the home; it actuates buyers and sellers in business, and lawyers in relation to clients, judge and jury. Lawmakers, clergymen, journalists, politicians are engaged in striving to affect the conduct of others in definite ways: to bring about *changes*, redirections, in conduct. There is a common *modus operandi* in all these cases. Certain objects are presented which it is thought will appeal to elements in the make-up of those addressed, so as to induce them to shape their action in a certain way, a way which in all probability they would not have taken if the object in question had not been held up to them as an end. These objects form what in the secondary and directly practical sense of the word are called motives. They are fundamentally important in attempts to influence the conduct of others. But moral theory has often committed a radical mistake in thinking of these objects which call out a change in the direction of action as if they were "motives" in the sense of originating movement or action. That theory logically terminates in making the self passive—as if stirred to action only from without.

§ 3. EGOISM AND ALTRUISM

Aside from the bearing of the right conception of motivation upon the unity of self and action, it is particularly important in connection with another problem. In British ethical theorizing this had been so much to the fore that Herbert Spencer called it the "crux of moral speculation." The problem is that of the relation of egoism and altruism, of self-regarding and other-regarding action, of self-love and benevolence. The issue concerns the motivation of *moral* action; discussion has been confused because of failure to examine the underlying problem of the nature of all motivation. This failure is perhaps most evident in those who have held that men are naturally moved only by self-love or regard for their own profit. But it has affected those who hold that men are actuated also by benevolent springs to action, and those who hold that benevolence is the sole motive which is morally justifiable.

A correct theory of motivation shows that both self-love and altruism are acquired dispositions, not original ingredients in our psychological make-up, and that each of them may be either morally good or morally reprehensible. Psychologically speaking, our native impulses and acts are neither egoistic nor altruistic; that is, they are not actuated by *conscious* regard for either one's own good or that of others. They are rather direct responses to situations. As far as self-love is concerned, the case is well stated by James. He says: "When I am moved by self-love to keep my seat while ladies stand, or grab something first and cut out my neighbor, what I really love is the seat; it is the thing itself which I grab. I love *them* primarily, as the mother loves her babe, or a generous man a heroic deed.

Whenever, as here, self-seeking is the outcome of simple instinctive propensity, it is but a name for certain reflex acts. Something rivets my attention and fatally provokes the 'selfish' response. . . . In fact the more thoroughly selfish I am in this primitive way, the more blindly absorbed my thought will be in the *objects* and impulses of my lust and the more devoid of any inward looking glance." [1] There is, in other words, no reflective quality, no deliberation, no conscious end, in such cases. An observer may look at the act and call it selfish, as in the case of the reaction of a parent to the child's grabbing of food. But in the beginning, this response signifies that the act is one which is *socially* objected to, so that reproof and instruction are brought to bear to induce the child in question to become conscious of the consequences of his act and to aim, *in the future*, at another kind of consequences.

The analysis of James applies equally well to so-called unselfish and benevolent acts—as is, indeed, suggested in the passage quoted in the statement about the mother's response to the needs of her babe. An animal that cares for its young certainly does so without thinking of their good and aiming consciously at their welfare. And the *human* mother in many instances "just loves," as we say, to care for her offspring; she may get as much satisfaction out of it as the "selfish" person does from grabbing a seat when he has a chance. In other words, there is a natural response to a particular situation, and one lacking in moral quality as far as it is wholly unreflective, not involving the idea of *any* end, good or bad.

An adult, however, observing acts of a child which, independently of their aim and "motive," show disregard or regard for others in their *results*, will reprove and approve. These acts tend to dissuade the child from one course of action and encourage him in the other. In that way the child gradually becomes conscious of himself and of others as beings who are

[1] *Principles of Psychology*, I., p. 320. The entire passage, pp. 317–329 should be consulted.

affected for good and evil, benefit and detriment, by his acts.
Conscious reference to one's own advantage and the good of
others may then become definitely a part of the *aim* of an act.
Moreover, the ideas of the two possibilities develop together.
One is aware of his own good as a definite end only as he
becomes aware of the contrasted good of others, and *vice versa*.
He thinks consciously of himself only in distinction from others,
as set over against them.

Selfishness and unselfishness in a genuinely moral sense thus
finally emerge, instead of being native "motives." This fact,
however, is far from implying that conscious regard for self
is morally bad and conscious regard for others is necessarily
good. Acts are not selfish because they evince consideration
for the future well-being of the self. No one would say that
deliberate care for one's own health, efficiency, progress in
learning is bad just because it is one's own. It is moral duty
upon occasion to look out for oneself in these respects. Such
acts acquire the quality of moral selfishness only when they
are indulged in so as to manifest obtuseness to the claims
of others. An act is not wrong because it advances the well-
being of the self, but because it is unfair, inconsiderate, in
respect to the rights, just claims, of others. Self-sustaining
and self-protective acts are, moreover, conditions of all acts
which are of service to others. Any moral theory which
fails to recognize the necessity of acting sometimes with
especial and conscious regard for oneself is suicidal; to
fail to care for one's health or even one's material well-being
may result in incapacitating one for doing anything for others.
Nor can it be argued that every one naturally looks out
for himself so that it is unnecessary to give thought to it.
It is as difficult to determine what is really good for oneself
as it is to discover just where the good of others lies and
just what measures will further it. It may even be asserted
that *natural* self-interest tends to blind us to what constitutes our own good, because it leads us to take a shortsighted

view of it, and that it is easier to see what is good for others, at least when it does not conflict with our own interests.

The real moral question is what *kind of* a self is being furthered and formed. And this question arises with respect to both one's own self and the selves of others. An intense emotional regard for the welfare of others, unbalanced by careful thought, may actually result in harm to others. Children are spoiled by having things done for them because of an uncontrolled "kindness"; adults are sometimes petted into chronic invalidism; persons are encouraged to make unreasonable demands upon others, and are grieved and hurt when these demands are not met; charity may render its recipients parasites upon society, etc. The goodness or badness of *consequences* is the main thing to consider, and these consequences are of the same nature whether they concern *my*self or *your*self. The kind of objects the self wants and chooses is the important thing; the *locus* of residence of these ends, whether in you or in me, cannot of itself make a difference in their moral quality.

The idea is sometimes advanced that action is selfish just because it manifests an interest, since every interest in turn involves the self. Examination of this position confirms the statement that everything depends upon the *kind* of self which is involved. It is a truism that all action springs from and affects a self, for *interest* defines the self. Whatever one is interested in is in so far a constituent of the self, whether it be collecting postage stamps, or pictures, making money, or friends, attending first nights at the theater, studying electrical phenomena, or whatever. Whether one obtains satisfaction by assisting friends or by beating competitors at whatever cost, the interest of the self is involved. The notion that therefore all acts are equally "selfish" is absurd. For "self" does not have the same significance in the different cases; there is always a self involved but the different selves have different values. A self changes its structure and its

value according to the kind of object which it desires and
seeks; according, that is, to the different kinds of objects in
which active interest is taken.

The identity of self and act, the central point in moral
theory, operates in two directions. It applies to the interpretation of the quality and value of the act and to that of the
self. It is absurd to suppose that the difference between the
good person and the bad person is that the former has no
interest or deep and intimate concern (leading to personal
intimate satisfaction) in what he does, while the bad person
is one who does have a personal stake in his actions. What
makes the difference between the two is the *quality* of the
interest that characterizes them. For the quality of the interest is dependent upon the nature of the object which arouses
it and to which it is attached, being trivial, momentous; narrow, wide; transient, enduring; exclusive, inclusive in exact
accord with the object. When it is assumed that because a
person acts from an interest, in and because its fulfillment
brings satisfaction and happiness, he therefore always acts
selfishly, the fallacy lies in supposing that there is a separation between the self and the end pursued. If there were, the
so-called end would in fact be *only* a means to bringing some
profit or advantage to the self. Now this sort of thing does
happen. A man may use his friends, for example, simply as
aids to his own personal advancement in his profession. But
in this case, he is *not* interested in them as friends or even as
human beings on their own account. He is interested in what
he can get out of them; calling them "friends" is a fraudulent
pretense. In short, the essence of the whole distinction between
selfishness and unselfishness lies in what sort of object the self
is interested. "Disinterested" action does not signify *un*-
interested; when it has this meaning, action is apathetic, dull,
routine, easily discouraged. The only intelligible meaning
that can be given to "disinterested" is that interest is intellectually fair, impartial, counting the same thing as of the

same value whether it affects my welfare or that of some one else.

So far we have been dealing with cases wherein action manifests and forms the self. In some of these cases the *thought* of the self definitely influences the passage of desire into choice and action. Thus we may say of an act that it manifests self-respect, or that it shows the agent to have no longer any sense of shame. The use of such terms as self-respect, sense of dignity, shame, in approbation is enough to show that conduct is not of necessity worse because the thought of self is a weighty factor in deciding what to do. When, however, we attribute an act to conceit or to false pride we disapprove. The conclusion, obviously, is that the issue is not whether the thought of self is a factor or not, but *what kind of self* is thought of, and in what way, to what purpose. Even "self-respect" is a somewhat ambiguous term. It may denote a sense of the dignity inhering in personality as such, a sense which restrains from doing acts which would besmirch it. It may mean respect for one's personal standing or repute in a community. Again, it may mean attachment to the family name which one bears, or a pride in some personal past achievement which one feels one must live up to. In the latter forms, it may be a definite support and safeguard to wise choice, or it may become a pretentious and hollow sham. It all depends, not on the general name employed, but on the constituents of the particular case. About the only general proposition which can be laid down is that the principle of equity and fairness should rule. The dividing line between, say, genuine and "false" pride is fixed by the equality or inequality of weight attached to the thought of one's own self in comparison with other selves. It is a matter of the intellectual attitude of objectivity and impartiality. The trouble with conceit, vanity, etc., is their warping influence on *judgment*. But humility, modesty, may be just as bad, since they too may destroy balance and equity of judgment.

Regard for others like regard for self has a double meaning. It may signify that action as a matter of fact contributes to the good of others, or it may mean that the *thought* of others' good enters as a determining factor into the conscious aim. In general, conduct, even on the conscious plane, is judged in terms of the elements of situations without explicit reference either to others or to oneself. The scholar, artist, physician, engineer, carries on the great part of his work without consciously asking himself whether his work is going to benefit himself or some one else. He is interested in the *work* itself; such objective interest is a condition of mental and moral health. It would be hard to imagine a situation of a more sickly sort than that in which a person thought that every act performed had to be actuated consciously by regard for the welfare of others; we should suspect the merchant of hypocrisy who claimed his motive in every sale was the good of his customer.

Nevertheless, there are occasions when *conscious* reference to the welfare of others is imperative. Somewhat curiously, at first appearance, this conscious reference is particularly needed when the immediate impulse is a sympathetic one. There is a strong natural impulse of resentment against an individual who is guilty of anti-social acts, and a feeling that retributive punishment of such a person is necessarily in the social interest. But the criterion of the interest actually served lies in its consequences, and there can be no doubt that much punishment, although felt to be in the interest of social justice, fosters a callous indifference to the common good, or even instills a desire in the one punished to get even in return by assailing social institutions. Compassion ranks ordinarily as a social motive-force. But one who consciously cultivates the emotion may find, if he will but consider results, that he is weakening the character of others, and, while helping them superficially, is harming them fundamentally.

Such statements do not signify, of course, that a passion

for justice or the emotion of pity should be suppressed. But just as the moral change in the person who thoughtlessly grabs something he wants is an expansion of interest to the thought of a wider circle of objects, so with the impulses which lie at the other pole. It is not easy to convert an immediate emotion into an interest, for the operation requires that we seek out indirect and subtle relations and consequences. But unless an emotion, whether labeled selfish or altruistic, is thus broadened, there is no reflective morality. To give way without thought to a kindly feeling is easy; to suppress it is easy for many persons; the difficult but needed thing is to retain it in all its pristine intensity while directing it, as a precondition of action, into channels of thought. A union of benevolent impulse and intelligent reflection is the interest most likely to result in conduct that is good. But in this union the rôle of thoughtful inquiry is quite as important as that of sympathetic affection.

§ 4. THE INCLUSIVE NATURE OF SOCIAL INTEREST

The discussion points to the conclusion that neither egoism nor altruism nor any combination of the two is a satisfactory principle. Selfhood is not something which exists apart from association and intercourse. The relationships which are produced by the fact that interests are formed in this social environment are far more important than are the adjustments of isolated selves. To a large extent, the emphasis of theory upon the problem of adjustment of egoism and altruism took place in a time when thought was decidedly individualistic in character. Theory was formed in terms of individuals supposed to be naturally isolated; social arrangements were considered to be secondary and artificial. Under such intellectual conditions, it was almost inevitable that moral theory should become preoccupied with the question of egoistic *versus* altruistic motivation. Since the prevailing individualism was expressed in an economic theory and practice which taught that each man was actuated by an exclusive regard for his own profit, moralists were led to insist upon the need of some check upon this ruthless individualism, and to accentuate the supremacy in *morals* (as distinct from business) of sympathy and benevolent regard for others. The ultimate significance of this appeal is, however, to make us realize the fact that regard for self and regard for others are both of them secondary phases of a more normal and complete interest: regard for the welfare and integrity of the social groups of which we form a part.

The family, for example, is something other than one person, plus another, plus another. It is an enduring form of association in which the members of the group stand from the beginning in relations to one another, and in which each member gets direction for his conduct by thinking of the whole group and his place in it, rather than by an adjustment of egoism and altruism. Similar illustrations are found in business, professional, and political associations. From the moral standpoint, the test of an industry is whether it serves the community as a whole, satisfying its needs effectively and fairly, while also providing the means of livelihood and personal development to the individuals who carry it on. This goal could hardly be reached, however, if the business man (a) thought exclusively of furthering his own interests; (b) of acting in a benevolent way toward others; or (c) sought some compromise between the two. In a justly organized social order, the very relations which persons bear to one another demand of the one carrying on a line of business the kind of conduct which meets the needs of others, while they also enable him to express and fulfill the capacities of his own being. Services, in other words, would be reciprocal and coöperative in their effect. We trust a physician who recognizes the social import of his calling and who is equipped in knowledge and skill, rather than one who is animated exclusively by personal affection no matter how great his altruistic zeal. The political action of citizens of an organized community will not be morally satisfactory unless they have, individually, sympathetic dispositions. But the value of this sympathy is not as a direct dictator of conduct. Think of any complex political problem and you will realize how short a way unenlightened benevolence will carry you. It has a value, but this value consists in power to make us attend in a broad way to all the social ties which are involved in the formation and execution of policies. Regard for self and regard for others should not, in other words, be *direct* motives to overt action. They should be forces which lead us to *think* of objects and consequences that would otherwise escape notice. These objects and consequences then constitute the *interest* which is the proper motive of action. Their stuff and material are composed of the relations which men actually sustain to one another in concrete affairs.

Interest in the social whole of which one is a member necessarily carries with it interest in one's own self. Every member of the group has his own place and work; it is absurd to suppose that this fact is significant in other persons but of little account in one's own case. To suppose that social interest is incompatible with concern for one's own health, learning, advancement, power of judgment, etc., is, literally, nonsensical. Since each one of us is a member of social groups and since the latter have no existence apart from the selves who compose them, there can be no effective social interest unless there is at the same time an intelligent regard for our own well-being and development. Indeed, there is a certain *primary* responsibility placed upon each individual in respect to his own power and growth. No community more backward and ineffective *as* a community can be imagined than one in which every member neglected his own concerns in order to attend to the affairs of his neighbors. When selfhood is taken for what it is, something existing in relationships to others and not in unreal isolation, independence of judgment, personal insight, integrity and initiative, become indispensable excellencies from the social point of view.

There is too often current a conception of charity which illustrates the harm which may accrue when objective social relations are shoved into the background. The giving of a kindly hand to a human being in distress, to numbers caught in a common catastrophe, is such a natural thing that it should almost be too much a matter of course to need laudation as a virtue. But the theory which erects charity in and of itself into a supreme excellence is a survival of a feudally stratified society, that is, of conditions wherein a superior class achieved merit by doing things gratuitously for an inferior class. The objection to this conception of charity is that it too readily becomes an excuse for maintaining laws and social arrangements which ought themselves to be changed in the interest of fair play and justice. "Charity" may even be used as a means for administering a sop to one's social conscience while at the same time it buys off the resentment which might otherwise grow up in those who suffer from social injustice. Magnificent philanthropy may be employed to cover up brutal economic exploitation. Gifts to libraries, hospitals, missions, schools may be employed as a means of rendering existing institutions more tolerable, and of inducing immunity against social change.

Again, deliberate benevolence is used as a means of keeping others dependent and managing their affairs for them. Parents, for example, who fail to pay due heed to the growing maturity of their children, justify an unjustifiable interference in their affairs, on the ground of kindly parental feelings. They carry the habits of action formed when children were practically helpless into conditions in which children both want and need to help themselves. They pride themselves on conduct which creates either servile dependence or bitter resentment and revolt in their offspring. Perhaps no better test case of the contrast between regard for personality bound up with regard for the realities of a social situation and abstract "altruism" can be found than is afforded in such an instance as this. The moral is not that parents should become indifferent to the well-being of their children. It is that *intelligent* regard for this welfare realizes the need for growing freedom with growing maturity. It displays itself in a change of the habits formed when regard for welfare called for a different sort of conduct. If we generalize the lesson of this instance, it leads to the conclusion that overt acts of charity and benevolence are incidental phases of morals, demanded under certain emergencies, rather than its essential principle. This is found in a constantly expanding and changing sense of what the concrete realities of human relations call for.

One type of moral theory holds up self-realization as the ethical ideal. There is an ambiguity in the conception which will serve to illustrate what has been said about the self. Self-realization may be the end in the sense of being an outcome and limit of right action, without being the end-in-*view*. The *kind* of self which is formed through action which is faithful to relations with others will be a fuller and broader self than one which is cultivated in isolation from or in opposition to the purposes and needs of others. In contrast, the kind of self which results from generous breadth of interest may be said alone to constitute a development and fulfillment of self, while the other way of life stunts and starves selfhood by cutting it off from the connections necessary to its growth. But to make self-realization a conscious aim might and probably would prevent full attention to those very relationships which bring about the wider development of self.

The case is the same with the interests of the self as with its realization. The final happiness of an individual resides in the supremacy of certain interests in the make-up of character; namely, alert, sincere, enduring interests in the objects in which all can share. It is found in such interests rather than in the accomplishment of definite external results because this kind of happiness alone is not at the mercy of circumstances. No amount of outer obstacles can destroy the happiness that comes from lively and ever-renewed interest in others and in the conditions and objects which promote their development. To those in whom these interests are alive (and they flourish to some extent in all persons who have not already been warped) their exercise brings happiness because it fulfills the self. They are not, however, preferred and aimed at *because* they give greater happiness, but as expressing the kind of self which a person fundamentally desires to be they constitute a happiness unique in kind.

The final word about the place of the self in the moral life is, then, that the very problem of morals is to form an original body of impulsive tendencies into a voluntary self in which desires and affections center in the values which are common; in which interest focusses in objects that contribute to the enrichment of the lives of all. If we identify the interests of such a self with the virtues, then we shall say, with Spinoza, that happiness is not the reward of virtue, but is virtue itself.

§ 5. RESPONSIBILITY AND FREEDOM

The ethical problems connected with the fact of selfhood culminate in the ideas of responsibility and freedom. Both ideas are bound up with far-reaching issues which have produced great controversy in metaphysics and religion as well as in morals. We shall consider them only with respect to the points in which these concepts are definitely connected with the analysis which precedes. So considered, an important side of responsibility has been already touched upon in connection with the transformation of native and psychological tendencies into traits of a self having moral significance and value.

Social demands and social approvals and condemnations are important factors in bringing about this change, as we had occasion to notice (p. 319). The point which is important is that they be used to produce a change in the attitude of those who are subject to them, especially the intellectual change of recognizing relations and meanings not hitherto associated with what they do. Now the commonest mistake in connection with the idea of responsibility consists in supposing that approval and reprobation have a retrospective instead of prospective bearing. The possibility of a desirable *modification* of character and the selection of the course of action which will make that possibility a reality is the central fact in responsibility. The child, for example, is at first held liable for what he has done, not because he deliberately and knowingly intended such action, but in order that *in the future* he may take into account bearings and consequences which he has failed to consider in what he *has* done. Here is where the human agent differs from a stone and inanimate thing, and indeed from animals lower in the scale.

It would be absurd to hold a stone responsible when it falls from a cliff and injures a person, or to blame the falling tree which crushes a passer-by. The reason for the absurdity is that such treatment would have and could have no conceivable influence on the future behavior of stone or tree. They do not interact with conditions about them so as to learn, so as to modify their attitudes and dispositions. A human being is held accountable in order that he may learn; in order that he may learn not theoretically and academically but in such a way as to modify and—to some extent—remake his prior self. The question of whether he might when he acted have acted differently from the way in which he did act is irrelevant. The question is whether he is capable of acting differently *next* time; the practical importance of effecting changes in human character is what makes responsibility important. Babes, imbeciles, the insane are not held accountable, because there is incapacity to learn and to change. With every increase of capacity to learn, there develops a larger degree of accountability. The fact that one did not deliberate before the performance of an act which brought injury to others, that he did not mean or intend the act, is of no significance, save as it may throw light upon the kind of response by others which will render him likely to deliberate next time he acts under similar circumstances. The fact that each act tends to *form*, through habit, a self which will perform a certain kind of acts, is the foundation, theoretically and practically of responsibility. We cannot undo the past; we can affect the future.

Hence responsibility in relation to control of our reactions to the conduct of others is twofold. The persons who employ praise and blame, reward and punishment, are responsible for the selection of those methods which will, with the greatest probability, modify in a desirable way the future attitude and conduct of others. There is no inherent principle of retributive justice that commands and justifies the use of reward and punishment independently of their consequences in each specific case. To appeal to such a principle when punishment breeds callousness, rebellion, ingenuity in evasion, etc., is but a method of refusing to acknowledge responsibility. Now the consequence which is most important is that which occurs in personal attitude: confirmation of a good habit, change in a bad tendency.

The point at which theories about responsibility go wrong is the attempt to base it upon a state of things which *precedes* holding a person liable, instead of upon what ensues in consequence of it. One is held responsible in order that he may *become* responsible, that is, responsive to the needs and claims of others, to the obligations implicit in his position. Those who hold others accountable for their conduct are themselves accountable for doing it in such a manner that this responsiveness develops. Otherwise they are themselves irresponsible in their own conduct. The ideal goal or limit would be that each person should be completely responsive in all his actions. But as long as one meets new conditions this goal cannot be reached; for where conditions are decidedly unlike those which one has previously experienced, one cannot be sure of the rightness of knowledge and attitude. Being held accountable by others is, in every such instance, an important safeguard and directive force in growth.

The idea of freedom has been seriously affected in theoretical discussions by misconceptions of the nature of responsibility. Those who have sought for an antecedent basis of and warrant for responsibility have usually located it in "freedom of the will," and have construed this freedom to signify an unmotivated power of choice, that is an arbitrary power to choose for no reason whatever except that the will does choose in this fashion. It is argued that there is no justice in holding a person liable for his act unless he might equally have done otherwise—completely overlooking the function of being held to account in improving his future conduct. A man might have "acted otherwise than he did act " *if* he had been a different kind of person, and the point in holding him liable for what he did do (and for being the kind of person he was in doing it) is that he may *become* a different kind of self and henceforth choose different sorts of ends.

In other words, freedom in its practical and moral sense (whatever is to be said about it in some metaphysical sense) is connected with possibility of growth, learning and modification of character, just as is responsibility. The chief reason we do not think of a stone as free is because it is not capable of changing its mode of conduct, of purposely readapting itself to new conditions. An animal such as a dog shows plasticity; it acquires new habits under the tutelage of others. But the dog plays a passive rôle in this change; he does not initiate and direct it; he does not become interested in it on its own account. A human being, on the other hand, even a young child, not only learns but is capable of being interested in learning, interested in acquiring new attitudes and dispositions. As we mature we usually acquire habits that are settled to the point of routine. But unless and until we get completely fossilized, we can break old habits and form new ones. No argument about causation can affect the fact, verified constantly in experience, that we can and do learn, and that the learning is not limited to acquisition of additional information but extends to remaking old tendencies. As far as a person becomes a different self or character he develops different desires and choices. Freedom in the practical sense develops when one is aware of this possibility and takes an interest in converting it into a reality. Potentiality of freedom is a native gift or part of our constitution in that we have *capacity* for growth and for being actively concerned in the process and the direction it takes. Actual or positive freedom is not a native gift or endowment but is acquired. In the degree in which we become aware of possibilities of development and actively concerned to keep the avenues of growth open, in the degree in which we fight against induration and fixity, and thereby realize the possibilities of recreation of our selves, we are actually free.

Except as the outcome of arrested development, there is no such thing as a fixed, ready-made, finished self. Every living self causes acts and is itself caused in return by what it does. All voluntary action is a remaking of self, since it creates new desires, instigates to new modes of endeavor, brings to light new conditions which institute new ends. Our personal identity is found in the thread of continuous development which binds together these changes. In the strictest sense, it is impossible for the self to stand still; it is becoming, and becoming for the better or the worse. It is in the *quality* of becoming that virtue resides. We set up this and that end to be reached, but *the* end is growth itself. To make an end a final goal is but to arrest growth. Many a person gets morally discouraged because he has not attained the object upon which he set his resolution, but in fact his moral status is determined by his movement in that direction, not by his possession. If such a person would set his thought and desire upon the *process* of evolution instead of upon some ulterior goal, he would find a new freedom and happiness. It is the next step which lies within our power.

It follows that at each point there is a distinction between an old, an accomplished self, and a new and moving self, between the static and the dynamic self. The former aspect is constituted by habits already formed. Habit gives facility, and there is always a tendency to rest on our oars, to fall back on what we have already achieved. For that is the easy course; we are at home and feel comfortable in lines of action that run in the tracks of habits already established and mastered. Hence, the old, the habitual self, is likely to be treated as if it were *the* self; as if new conditions and new demands were something foreign and hostile. We become uneasy at the idea of initiating new courses; we are repelled by the difficulties that attend entering upon them; we dodge assuming a new responsibility. We tend to favor the old self and to make its perpetuation the standard of our valuations and the end of our conduct. In this way, we withdraw from actual conditions and their requirements and opportunities; we contract and harden the self.

The growing, enlarging, liberated self, on the other hand, goes forth to meet new demands and occasions, and readapts and remakes itself in the process. It welcomes untried situations. The necessity for choice between the interests of the old and of the forming, moving, self is recurrent. It is found at every stage of civilization and every period of life. The civilized man meets it as well as the savage; the dweller in the slums as well as the person in cultivated surroundings; the "good" person as well as the "bad." For everywhere there is an opportunity and a need to go beyond what one has been, beyond "himself," if the self is identified with the body of desires, affections, and habits which has been potent in the past. Indeed, we may say that the good person is precisely the one who is most conscious of the alternative, and is the most concerned to find openings for the newly forming or growing self; since no matter how "good" he has been, he becomes "bad" (even though acting upon a relatively high plane of attainment) as soon as he fails to respond to the demand for growth. Any other basis for judging the moral status of the self is conventional. In reality, direction of movement, not the plane of attainment and rest, determines moral quality.

Practically all moralists have made much of a distinction between a lower and a higher self, speaking of the carnal and spiritual, the animal and the truly human, the sensuous and the rational, selves which exist side by side in man and which war with one another. Moralists have often supposed that the line between the two selves could be drawn once for all and upon the basis of definite qualities and traits belonging respectively to one and the other. The only distinction, however, that can be drawn without reducing morals to conventionality, self-righteous complacency, or a hopeless and harsh struggle for the unattainable, is that between the attained static, and the moving, dynamic self. When there is talk of the lower animal self, and so on, it is always by *contrast*, not on the basis of fixed material. A self that was truly moral under a set of former conditions may become a sensuous, appetitive self when it is confronted with a painful need for developing new attitudes and devoting itself to new and difficult objectives. And, contrariwise, the higher self is that formed by the step in advance of one who *has* been living on a low plane. As he takes the step he enters into an experience of freedom. If we state the moral law as the injunction to each self on every possible occasion to identify the self with a new growth that is possible, then obedience to law is one with moral freedom.

In concluding the theoretical discussion of this part, we sum up by stating the point of view from which all the different problems and ideas have been looked at. For this point of view it is, which supplies the unifying thread: *Moral conceptions and processes grow naturally out of the very conditions of human life.* (1) Desire belongs to the intrinsic nature of man; we cannot conceive a human being who does not have wants, needs, nor one to whom fulfillment of desire does not afford satisfaction. As soon as the power of thought develops, needs cease to be blind; thought looks ahead and foresees results. It forms purposes, plans, aims, ends-in-view. Out of these universal and inevitable facts of human nature there necessarily grow the moral conceptions of the Good, and of the value of the intellectual phase of character, which amid all the conflict of desires and aims strives for insight into the inclusive and enduring satisfaction: wisdom, prudence.

(2) Men live together naturally and inevitably in society; in companionship and competition; in relations of coöperation and subordination. These relations are expressed in demands, claims, expectations. One person has the conviction that fulfillment of his demands by others is his *right;* to these others it comes as an *obligation*, something owed, due, to those who assert the claim. Out of the interplay of these claims and obligations there arises the general concept of Law, Duty, Moral Authority, or Right.

(3) Human beings approve and disapprove, sympathize and resent, as naturally and inevitably as they seek for the objects they want, and as they impose claims and respond to them. Thus the moral Good presents itself neither merely as that which satisfies desire, nor as that which fulfills obligation, but as that which is *approvable*. From out of the mass of phenomena of this sort there emerge the generalized ideas of Virtue or Moral Excellence and of a Standard which regulates the manifestation of approval and disapproval, praise and blame.

Special phenomena of morals change from time to time with change of social conditions and the level of culture. The facts of desiring, purpose, social demand and law, sympathetic approval and hostile disapproval are constant. We cannot imagine them disappearing as long as human nature remains human nature, and lives in association with others. The fundamental conceptions of morals are, therefore, neither arbitrary nor artificial. They are not imposed upon human nature from without but develop out of its own operations and needs. Particular aspects of morals are transient; they are often, in their actual manifestation, defective and perverted. But the framework of moral conceptions is as permanent as human life itself.

LITERATURE

For self in general, see Bosanquet, *Psychology of the Moral Self,* 1897; Otto, *Things and Ideals,* 1924, ch. vi.; Cooley, *Human Nature and the Social Order,* 1922, chs. v.–ix.; Dewey, *Human Nature and Conduct,* 1922, pp. 134–139 and see Index. The conception of altruism under that name was introduced by Comte. See his *System of Positive Politics,* Introduction, ch. iii., and Part II., trans. 1854, ch. ii.; a good summary is contained in Levy-Bruhl's *Philosophy of Comte,* trans. 1903, Book IV.; see Spencer, *Principles of Ethics,* Vol. I., Part I., chs. xi.–xiv.; Stephen, *Science of Ethics,* 1882, ch. vi.; Sorley, *Recent Tendencies in Ethics,* 1904; Sidgwick, *Methods of Ethics,* 1901, pp. 494–507, Adler, *An Ethical Philosophy of Life,* 1918; Hastings' *Dictionary of Religion and Ethics,* 1922, article on " Altruism"; Sharp, *Ethics,* 1928, ch. v., on self-sacrifice, chs. xxii. and xxiii.; H. E. Davis, *Tolstoy and Nietzsche,* 1927; Calkins, *The Good Man, and The Good,* 1918.

On freedom and responsibility, Sharp, *Ethics,* 1928, ch. xiii.; James, *Will to Believe,* 1915, essay on " Dilemma of Determinism "; G. E. Moore, *Ethics,* 1912, ch. vi.; *Freedom in the Modern World,* 1928, edited by H. M. Kallen, especially Essays i., iii., x., xi., xii.; Dewey, *Human Nature and Conduct,* 1922, pp. 303–317; Everett, *Moral Values,* 1918, ch. xxi.; Stapledon, *A Modern Theory of Ethics,* 1929, ch. xi. On self-interest, see Mandeville, *Fable of Bees.*

Sidgwick, *Methods of Ethics,* 1901, Book I., ch. vii. and Book II., ch. v. Self-realization: Wright, *Self-Realization,* 1913; Aristotle, *Ethics;* Green, *Prolegomena to Ethics,* 1890 (for criticism of Green, see Dewey, *Philosophical Review,* Vol. II., pp. 652–664); Palmer, *The Nature of Goodness,* 1903.

INDEX

Agathon, 92

Altruism, theory of, 156–163; dangers of, 158f., 166

Approbation, as central concept, 27; and Ch. IV; its native quality, 89f.; and virtue, 91; and standards, 92–94; utilitarian theory of, 98ff.; as a moral force, 109; as social, 151, 168f.

Aristotle, referred to, 44, 58; on judgment of good, 131; on character, 150

Arnold, M., 12

Asceticism, and cynics, 52; as the end, 51–56, 62

Association, a necessary fact, 164

Attitude. *See* Character, Habit

Authority, in morals, 26; Ch. III, *passim*, esp. 66, 68f.

Bain, on pleasure as end, 38

Benevolence, as standard, 95ff. *See* Sympathy

Bentham, Jeremy, on intention, 16, 19; 92f.; criticized by Mill, 98–100; 127

Business, moral problems of, 118

Carlyle, Thomas, 107

Casuistry, 138f.

Categorical imperative. *See* Kant

Changes, social, moral effects of, 20, 23

Character, as stable, 9; and conduct, 10–15; central, 15; and intent, 18; as criterion of pleasures, 40f.; and moral judgment, 131ff.; and end, 96–100; analyzed, 8–10; continuity of, 11

Charity, misconception of, 166

Chastity, and cultus, 21

Choice, 148f.; and self, 149f.

Coercion, 9, 69, 77

Conduct, in relation to character, 10–18; involves continuity, 11ff., 74

Conflicts, 19, 22, occasion of reflection, 6f., 59; of desires, 36ff.; and choice, 148ff.

Conformism, 84

Conscience, and reflective morals, 3f.; nature of, 121; analyzed, 132–136

Conscientiousness, true and false, 120. *See* Judgment, Moral

Consequences, and motive, 16f., 39, 72–77, 105ff.; in utilitarianism, 98ff.; and self, 148ff.

Courage, 117

Criterion, moral, 27f. *See* Standard, Utilitarianism

Custom, and reflection, 5f.

Cynics, 52

Deliberation, nature of, 162–166; and the self, 134; and imagination, 135; and conflict of impulses, 148f.

Democracy, nature of, 168

Desire, in relation to thought, 32ff. *See* Good, The

Discipline, 56

Disinterestedness, 49, 160

Dogmatism, evils of, 127

Duty, 70–76, Ch. III; social claims, 68–70; justification of, 77–84; generalized sense of, 85ff.; and a social office, 81

Education, 98

Egoism, 156–163. *See* Self, Selfishness

Eliot, George, 46

Emerson, on abstinence, 59

Empiricism. *See* Intuitionalism

Ends, and the Good, 25, 32–37; teleological morals, 27; as central concept, Ch. I; and reflection, 29ff.; analyzed, 31ff.; and pleasure, 37–45; and desire, 32f.; and wisdom, 37; relation to standard, 46, 101ff.; and success, 50; and asceticism, 51–56; objective interests, 56–58; and the self, 158ff.

Epicureans, 47–50, 54, 59

Equality, 94, 114

Esthetic factors, moral influence of, 59, 92, 130
Ethics, 25–28; theories of, Ch. I
Expediency, 58

Friendship, 48, 69

Goethe, 35f.
Golden Rule, 22, 97, 141f.
Goldsmith, O., 14
Good, The, hedonism defined and criticized, 37–47, Ch. II; as happiness, 45ff.; related to wisdom, 37; Epicurean theory of, 47–50; as conquest of passion, 51–56; as objective interests, 56–62; conflict of, 59–65; in utilitarianism, 98ff.; double meaning of, 123; natural and moral, 103
Goodness. *See* Virtue

Habit, 53, 57; and the self, 13f.; and purpose, 30f.; as moral stay, 53f.; and objective interest, 57f. *See* Character, Conduct
Happiness, its constitution, 45ff., 167; and personal disposition, 97ff., 103; and desire, 102; private and common, 103f. *See* Utilitarianism
Hazlitt, on pleasure and the Good, 42
Hedonism, criticized, 37–47, 152; theory of ends of desire confused with theory of standards, 94f.; paradox of, 102
Herbert, G., 133
Honesty, as policy, 50
Humanitarianism, 94
Hume, D., 92
Hypocrisy, 113

Ideal, nature of, 133
Indifference, of acts, 9f., 12
Individualism, and justice, 106f.; as theory, 163
Inhibition, nature of, 34f., 54f.
Intention, place of in morals, 8f.; analysis of, 16f. *See* Ends, Motive
Interests, and the Good, 56–58; and motives, 153ff.; and the self, 159f.; as social, 163–168
Intuitionalism, 93, 120; truth and error in, 124–127, 135; as immediate sensitivity, 127f.; defect, 141
Isolation, of the moral, 121

James, William, on passion and thought, 33; on moral excercise, 53, 55; on self love, 156f.
Judgment, moral, Ch. V; its object, 34; as separate faculty, 67; as practical and theoretical, 90; and sympathy, 107, 124f.; and the self, 150. *See* Intuitionalism, Wisdom
Jural influence, of morals, 27
Justice, and standard, 105–109; as virtue, 116; legalistic view of, 109

Kalon, and *Kalokagathos*, 92, 131
Kant, subordinates good to law, 70ff.; separation of motive and consequences, 16, 72; duty as universal and particular, 73f.; on knowledge, 120f.; on good will, 147
Knowledge, Ch. V; of persons, 129; will to know, 143

Laissez faire, 106
Law, moral, duty, Ch. III
Legalism, 109, 139. *See* Jural influence, Law, Right
Liberty, nature of, 171ff. *See* Individualism
Locke, referred to, 53, 140
Loyalty, Ch. III

Measure, 59
Mill, John Stuart, on sources of value, 57; on expediency, 58; on pleasures as end, 38; on their quality, 43f.; his interest in personal character, 94ff.
Millay, E. St. Vincent, 47
Milton, 55
Moral Sense School. *See* Intuitionalism
Morality, reflective, Ch. I, 89ff., 109f., 112–118, 124, 162; not isolated, 65f., 67f.; as servile, 78; as intrinsic in life, 174ff. *See* Theory, moral
Mores. *See* Custom
Motives, and intention, 17; analyzed, 18; pleasure as, 41; their nature, 151–156; relation to interests, 153; self-love as, 156ff. *See* Consequences

Nature, Roman law of, 70
Non-conformity, 84

Obligations, Ought, Oughtness. *See* Duty

Personality, as end in itself, 75. *See* Individuality

Plato, on the Good, 9–14; on teaching virtue, 4; emphasis on knowledge, 120

Pleasure, hedonistic theory, 37–47; present and future, 39–41; Hazlitt on, 42; and character, 40–42; higher and lower, 44; and happiness, 45ff.; in utilitarianism, 94–100

Praise. *See* Approbation

Precedent, 136

Principles, nature of, 85, 136–142; difference from rules, 137ff.

Problems of moral theory, 5, 20, 25–28, 87

Punishment. *See* Justice

Puritans, referred to, 52, 139

Reason, in Kant, 73f.; double meaning of, 67f.

Reform, moral, 58f.

Responsibility, its nature, 168ff.; and character, 169f.; and consequences, 170f.; and freedom, 171

Right, the, as basic concept, Ch. III; relation to good, 64f., 77; relation to ends, 65f.; social origin of, 68–70, 79–80; Kantian theory of, 70–76; justification of, 77–85; generalized sense of, 85–88. *See* Duty, Law, Reason

Rules, as fixed and principles, 139ff.

Santayana, G., 61

Science, and moral progress, 23f., 144

Self, place in morals, Ch. VI; and choice, 147–151; and act, 150f., 160; and motives, 151–156, 172–174. *See* Character

Self-interest, 50, 158

Selfishness, in Kant, 71; nature of, 157–160

Self-realization, 167

Self-sacrifice, 35

Sense. *See* Intuitionalism

Shaftesbury, 92

Smith, Adam, 92

Social Environment, moral significance of, 145; influence, on ends, 61; on duty, 87; on virtue, 117

Socrates, 5

Spencer, Herbert, 106, 156

Standard, and approbation, Ch. IV; and praise and blame, 91–94; in utilitarianism, 94–100; relation to ends, 101ff., 142; as justice and benevolence, 104–109; revision of, 132f., 145

Stephen, L., quoted, on character, 15–16

Success, as an end, 50–51, 89

Sympathetic resentment, 89

Sympathy, as basis of approval, 93ff.; Mill and Bentham on, 99f.; as emotional and intellectual, 107, 129f., 164f.

Teleological Theories, 27. *See* Ends, Good

Temptation, 6, 10

Theory, moral, nature of, Ch. I; and reflective morals, 5–8; and conflict, 5; value and limitations of, 7ff.; present need of, 20ff.; sources of, 22–25; problems, classified, 25–28; schools of, 24ff.; hedonistic, 37–47; Epicurean, 47–50; ascetic, 51–56; Kantian, 71–77; utilitarian, 93–100; egoistic and altruistic, 156–163; intuitional, 124–135

Toleration, 84

Utilitarianism, as theory of standard of approbation, 93ff.; confusion with hedonism, 94–100; emphasis on wide sympathy, 94; transformed by J. S. Mill, 96–100; and social reform, 107f.; criticized, 150

Value, conflicts of, 5, 59; material and ideal, 131f.; judgments of, 122. *See* Approbation, Good, Judgment

Vice. *See* Virtue

Virtue, as wisdom, 37f.; in relation to praise and blame, Ch. IV, *passim*, especially, 91, 101, 109f.; traits of, 112–118; relation to custom, 112; defined, 113; unity of, 115

Voluntary action. *See* Character, Choice, Desire, Ends, Will

War, as moral problem, 6, 22

Will, meaning of "strong," 36. *See* Choice, Habit

Wisdom, Epicureans on, 47ff.; different theories of, Ch. I

Worth. *See* Value

Wrong, the, as disloyalty, 81f.